WAKING NIGHTMARE

WAKING NIGHTMARE

BY CARLY ANNE WEST

ART BY TIM HEITZ AND ARTFUL DOODLERS LTD.

Scholastic Inc.

All rights reserved. Published by Scholastic Inc., *Publishers since 1920.* SCHOLASTIC and associated logos are trademarks and/or registered trademarks of Scholastic Inc.

The publisher does not have any control over and does not assume any responsibility for author or third-party websites or their content.

No part of this publication may be reproduced, stored in a retrieval system, or transmitted in any form or by any means, electronic, mechanical, photocopying, recording, or otherwise, without written permission of the publisher. For information regarding permission, write to Scholastic Inc., Attention: Permissions Department, 557 Broadway, New York, NY 10012.

ISBN 978-1-338-28909-1

10 9 8 7 6 5 4 3 2 1   19 20 21 22 23
Printed in the U.S.A. 23

First printing 2019
Interior design by Cheung Tai

PROLOGUE

'm running so fast the pine needles barely pierce my feet. It doesn't matter, though. Whatever's behind me is gaining. I can hear its breath catching in its throat, the delicious scream it's dying to let fly once it has me in its grasp.

I pump my arms harder, leaning forward into the dark thicket of trees. Twisting blackberry vines reach for my ankles and tear at my shins with their thorns. The leaves are slick with fresh rain, and my feet keep slipping, but I can't stop. I have to get there first.

Over the snarls and grunts of the thing that pursues me, I finally hear it: the faint, tinny sound of carnival music. I'm close.

Just above the tree line, I spy the shadow of a Ferris wheel basket. I press on and pick up speed, tumbling through a clearing and clambering into the rocking Ferris wheel car. I shut the door tight, a split second before the beast slams into the side, sending my car swinging as I rise up. Up. Up.

I'm above the forest now, and I can see every charred

remnant of the Golden Apple Amusement Park. For a moment, I see it as it was—freshly painted signs and polished rides, the sounds of kids squealing and people laughing, their joyful cries carried high on a breeze that turns quickly to a cold chill once I'm at the peak of the Ferris wheel's cycle. But when I look down, I see I'm no longer in an enclosed cage; I'm in a grocery cart, its metal grid pressing icy impressions into the backs of my legs.

I look through the cart's slats at the park, its brightness corroded in oily residue and angry graffiti. The beast that chased me here is nowhere to be found, but something else catches my eye—a glint of metal just beyond the crooked trees at the edge of the park.

I wait until I'm low and let the cart tip me to the ground, leaving behind the canned carnival tune, edging past the decaying wood and distorted, shadowy remains of popcorn booths. Beyond the mechanical graveyard stands the skeleton of the Rotten Core roller coaster, one lonely car at its apex, the rest of its cars missing. The dead ride looms impossibly tall in the dark of this long night, and now is when I want to wake up.

Wake up, Nicky. This isn't real.

But that's never worked before, and somehow I know that it definitely won't work tonight because somewhere in the wreckage of the Rotten Core is a secret I'm supposed to uncover.

"I just want to go home," I say aloud, even though there's no one here to answer. The beast has wandered elsewhere in search of me. The park long silent to the pleas of frightened kids.

The gleam that enticed me from the Ferris wheel and toward the roller coaster winks at me again, and this time I see exactly where it's coming from: directly under the tree where they found Lucy Yi after the accident, her body curled tight at the bottom of the roller coaster car.

I walk toward it slowly, certain that whatever lured me here needs to be found.

But I don't want to find it.

The moonlight makes the metal glow silver, but I know the bracelet I'm looking at—the delicate chain with its dancing apple charm—isn't silver. It's gold. I crouch to look at it, turn the charm over in my shaking hand, but I already know the inscription that I'll find there.

GOLDEN APPLE YOUNG INVENTORS CLUB

I pull the bracelet from the dirt and expect it to come free, but it catches on something underneath. I pull harder; the bracelet won't budge. I swipe at the dirt beside it and try to find what it's caught on, and the ground around it grows softer. Soon, I'm moving clumps of mud from the chain threaded through my fingers.

I pull one last time on the chain, and to my horror, a pale hand pries free from the dirt.

It grasps me hard by the wrist, and I try to break away, but its grip on me is fierce. I lean back, and it leans with me, pulling itself from the bowels of the park.

Its arm emerges first, bent at an unnatural angle, then another arm to match it. It grips me harder, its mud-caked fingers pressing so deep into my skin, I think my wrist might break. The other hand palms the ground, looking for leverage to bring the rest of whatever lies beneath to the surface.

"HELP!" I scream, but it's no use.

The thing is coming, and there's no stopping it now.

Its head begins to rise, brown sludge and worms and beetles sliding away from its smooth, pale face. Just as it lifts its head to mine, it reaches its other arm for me.

Chapter 1

I open my eyes to a cloudy moon, the kind they always show in werewolf movies right before some unsuspecting guy turns into a bloodthirsty monster. Smears of clouds waft in front of the silver light, and I can't remember the last time I got to see the moon this clearly, even through the clouds.

The wonder of that moon fades fast as I brush away the pinpricks that are poking into my back. They're pine needles. I sit up too fast, seeing a thousand circling moons for a second before my vision finds its way back.

I'm on the ground, and I'm certain I've been on this ground before. I've never slept on this ground before, though. Never in my wildest dreams would I do that. Well, maybe in my wildest dreams I *would*, because somehow I got to the Golden Apple Amusement Park.

I stand slowly, my body stiff and shivering, and it's no wonder. It's the middle of December, and I'm standing in the forest in flannel pajamas and bare feet. Sure, the real winter weather hasn't landed yet, but I'm not exactly in outdoor gear. The wind swirls in tight circles around me, and I throw my arms around myself, but not before I notice the clumps of dirt crusted to my hands and buried under my fingernails. A violent shiver works its way down my spine as I remember those hands from my nightmare—the dirt I unburied them from.

I look at my own hands again, then search the ground beside me. There, in a pile maybe three feet from where I inexplicably made my bed last night, is a mound of soil beside a small hole. I edge toward the hole, bracing myself to fight off whatever lies in wait for me, but as I stand over the pile, I see the hole is empty. I search my hands one more time for a clue as to how I got here and what I was apparently doing in my sleep.

My hands tell me nothing except that I'm freezing.

I turn toward the only path I know for getting home: the path I used to walk with Aaron when we would come back from the Golden Apple factory.

Before Aaron disappeared.

Aaron Peterson was the first friend I made when we moved to Raven Brooks last summer. He liked picking locks and I liked building gadgets and together we served up justice to hoity-toity grocery store owners and inconsiderate dog owners alike. My family has never stayed in one town for long; it's been hard for my dad to hold down a job. Aaron made me hope we would stay put for a while.

He was the first person I met who was as weird as I am. But where my family is quirky at best, Aaron's family was . . . strange.

His dad, Theodore Masters Peterson, was the famed—and troubled—inventor who engineered the Golden Apple Amusement Park, the last in a line of theme parks that had seen their share of disaster. Aaron's mom, Diane, died in a car accident at the end of the summer . . . something that tore their family apart. And Aaron's little sister, Mya, had stood with me in this very park four months ago, begging me for help.

I half run, half walk home, the cold and my raw feet keeping me from moving as fast as I want to. I feel a vague stinging along my ankles, and when I lift my pant legs, I find a series of fresh scrapes etched across my skin, the telltale wounds of blackberry thorns.

By the time I get home, the moon has mostly disappeared behind its protective clouds, and though the streetlights are still on, I know they won't be for long. I'm shivering so hard, I can hardly make it up the trellis and through the window to my room.

"So that's how I got out," I mutter once I'm safely inside. And that would make sense. Of course I would sneak out the window. It's not like I'm going to chance waking my parents by sauntering out the front door in the middle of the night. Even in my sleep, I must have known better.

But why would I sneak out? Why would I leave in my pajamas? What could I possibly have been looking for?

"And why can't I remember any of it?"

I stand where I am by my window and search for clues, for any sign at all that I was sleepwalking for a reason, that I'm not completely out of my mind. I see nothing to comfort me, though. The bedsheets are thrown back like I had been sleeping at some point. My desk lamp is on, and while my desk is clear, I know that it wasn't earlier that night. It never is.

I walk slowly to the desk and pull out the middle drawer, the deepest one. I slide the pencil tray out of the way and lift the tiny tab fastened to the back of the drawer, revealing its false bottom. Setting the pencil tray and plywood aside, I remove the face of the bottom drawer—the decoy drawer—and lift from it the heavy gray binder, its contents spilling out the sides and torn at the edges.

Then I turn to the last page I remember studying before I went to sleep last night. It was a newer article, the latest in the saga of what will happen to the property on which the Golden Apple Amusement Park still sits.

There's a picture of the old WELCOME sign at the Golden Apple Amusement Park, the black-and-blue graffiti looking like a bruise across its face. The right half of the sign has been burned away, leaving only the WELC, and the face of the dancing golden apple has been so disfigured, I find myself wishing it had been burned away, too.

Below that picture are two I've already seen—the school picture of Lucy Yi, her head tilted as she smiles, her wrist decorated with the Golden Apple Young Inventors Club bracelet, and the camera-wary Mr. Peterson, his palm blocking the flash.

A date has been set for the long-anticipated hearing over what to do with the land that once housed Raven Brooks's famed amusement park. On December 28, a judge will hear arguments from lawyers representing the landowner, Raven Brooks Municipal Bank and Trust, which took ownership after the Golden Apple Corporation went bankrupt, and lawyers representing EarthPro, a land and business development firm interested in purchasing the land that has stood for years as a reminder of the tragedy that befell a family and a former hometown business.

In a case that has pitted neighbor against neighbor, argument over the land involves the question of what will be done with the ruins of the amusement park and the abandoned factory that resides nearby. Yet as the people of Raven Brooks know, feelings run deeper than a feud over land.

"If I were Brenda Yi, I'd be rooting for EarthPro all the way. After what happened to her daughter, I don't know how she's lived with those ruins as a constant reminder," says Eddie Reisman, a physical therapist at Raven Brooks Bones and Joints.

Sally Unger, a cosmetology student, disagrees. "Look, what happened to that poor girl was a tragedy, but selling the land to another faceless corporation? What's that going to solve? It's just going to push all the local businesses out of town!"

Still, others struggle with the question of culpability. Says Herb Villanueva, owner of Buzzy's Coffee Stand in the Square, "I still don't like how nobody was ever really to blame, you know? I mean, yeah, the Golden Apple people paid out the nose, and I guess that's something, but c'mon. We all know who built those rides. No one wants to be the one to say it, but let's just say there's someone still walking free who hasn't had to answer for his part in the whole mess."

I stop reading because I've read it all a million times. I know the story before it hits the papers, before the people at Tillman's natural grocer or the Square or the university are talking about it. Dad talks about it at home to Mom. Maritza talks about it to Enzo. Strangers talk to strangers about it. It's all anyone talks about anymore in Raven Brooks.

I flip past the pages and pages of articles I've kept, eyeing the places I've highlighted, any mention of Mr. Peterson's career. I skip past all the clippings and move on to the graph paper where I've broken the page into careful columns, dates separated by hourly blocks, color-coded with different highlighters so I can easily distinguish actions.

There's no other way to put it, the standing. It's the wandering from his house, the lingering in his front yard. It's him crossing the street to stare up at my window. He does it enough to warrant a highlighter assignment.

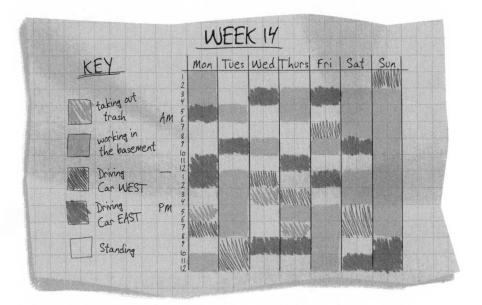

I flip to the back of the binder, the back flap bulging under its contents. I slide my index finger and thumb inside and pull out the gold chain with its apple charm. I turn it over and over in my hand, tarnish greening it slowly, but I don't need to be able to read the inscription any more than I need to read all the newspaper articles about the land and the lawsuit.

I still read them, though. I read them looking for any mention at all of Aaron or Mya, of where they've gone and why nobody cares.

Because that's the truth: Nobody cares. I've been watching the Peterson house for 107 days, and I've seen no trace of Aaron or Mya. It was easy enough to distract myself at first—Enzo's video game collection and Trinity's encyclopedic knowledge of Raven Brooks ensured we became fast friends, and Enzo's younger sister, Maritza, has been nice to me . . . if not exactly forthcoming about her own friendship with Mya.

During the first month of school, people told me to leave it alone, but no matter how much I tried not to worry, with every day that passed my skin felt a little tighter. Until the news finally came in November: Aaron and Mya were shipped off to live with a relative hundreds of miles away.

The strain of the loss must have been too much, Dad told me. *It's probably for the best.*

But every night in my dreams, my mind takes me back to the Golden Apple Amusement Park.

To the bracelet I found at the bottom of my trellis.

To the note with the smear of blood.

To the fear in Mya's voice in that home movie I found in the factory.

Because, if Aaron and Mya are safe somewhere, why can't I shake the feeling that I failed them?

Chapter 2

I showered last night, but I woke up in such a fog this morning, I don't remember if I put on deodorant, which of course makes me sweat more.

I find a secluded spot behind a tree in the quad and do a quick sniff check under my shirt. When I emerge, still unconvinced, Maritza is standing in front of me, eyes narrowed in suspicion.

"You've looked better," she says, a giggle just barely hidden in her voice. "You smell fine, though."

That makes me sweat even more. Maritza has been hanging out with Enzo, Trinity, and me a lot more since school started back in session three months ago. She's cute and all, but she's Enzo's sister, so that makes it weird. That doesn't stop my glands from getting all Pavlovian around her, though. Seriously, did I remember to put on deodorant or not?

"Where's Enzo?" I ask her, fleeing from the topic of my body odor.

"'Practicing,'" she says, her fingers twitching in air quotes as we head for our lockers.

"Right, basketball," I say, trading one uncomfortable topic for another.

"So, when are you going to tell him?" she asks.

"Tell him what?"

She arches her eyebrow. "That you hate it."

"I don't *hate* basketball," I say defensively.

"Okay, that you have zero intention of trying out," she says.

And this time, I can't disagree.

"It's . . . complicated," I say.

She smiles but keeps her eyes on the hallway in front of us. "Is it? I mean, I'm pretty sure it could go something like, 'Hey, you gonna try out for basketball?' 'Nah, I'm not really into sports.' 'Oh, okay.'"

I try to smile, but I think I only manage something resembling a grimace.

"Right. Easy as that," I say.

"Just like that," she agrees. Then we're quiet because we both know it's far from simple.

I leave out the part where Enzo suddenly developed an interest in basketball around the same time Aaron and Mya magically vanished. And Maritza leaves out how quickly the entire town was willing to buy the lame story Mr. Peterson gave them about how he sent his kids to live with an aunt out of state.

And neither of us mentions how weird things have gotten

in Raven Brooks now that the bank wants to sell the land that used to belong to the Golden Apple Corporation to EarthPro, and some people like my mom think that's great for the local economy, and other people like crazy Mrs. Tillman have the not-so-crazy idea that their small businesses could be in trouble.

None of that should have anything to do with Enzo's sudden interest in basketball, but the timing is more than a little suspicious. Something I hadn't realized until recently is just how close the Espositos are to the Yi family. It seems people can't bring up poor Lucy Yi without remembering how close she was with Maritza and Mya. That puts Enzo in uncomfortable company with Aaron and Mr. Peterson. And suddenly, with the death of Diane Peterson and EarthPro's interest in the Golden Apple Corporation's land, the name Peterson is back on everyone's lips. It's no wonder Enzo wants to blend into a different crowd, one that nobody can associate with tragedy.

Anyway, that's what I tell myself when I'm trying not to worry that Enzo considers me social kryptonite.

Yeah . . . complicated.

By the time the first bell rings, I've all but forgotten about how I smell, instead finding myself in familiar territory: thoughts of Aaron and Mya.

Because no matter what happens with Enzo and basketball or the Golden Apple land that EarthPro wants now, it all leads back to Aaron and Mya. How everyone is so willing to take Mr. Peterson at his word that his kids are fine, and in the same breath blame him for the death of Lucy Yi.

The final bell buzzes just as Ruben and Seth duck into the room, Enzo trailing behind them. Enzo's new friends are each about half a foot taller than him, and they also seem entirely unaware that Enzo is friends with them, even though they all wear their hair in the same gelled, slicked-back style, making it look like they're wearing matching lacquer helmets. Ruben and Seth grab the last two seats next to each other, leaving Enzo to shuffle past me to the back of the class.

Just as he lowers his bag to the ground, the basketball he was juggling bounces and rolls to the front of the room, hitting a perturbed Mr. Pierce on the toe of his worn black shoe.

"Mr. Esposito, let's leave the ball on the field, shall we?" Mr. Pierce says, nudging the ball back down the aisle.

The class snickers. Mr. Pierce is the only other person who cares less about basketball than I do.

Ruben and Seth laugh a little longer than everyone else, and I hope Enzo doesn't see them sneaking glances over their shoulders at him.

I peel the perforated margin from my notebook paper and ball it up, flicking it at the back of Seth's head.

He whips around, eyeing the rest of us, and I get really interested in my integer homework.

By the end of the day, my sleepless night has caught up with me, and I can barely keep my eyes open. I'm dragging my backpack on the ground, but I don't care. I just want to get home.

"Man, you look like you've been sleeping with the llamas," Enzo says, and Trinity shoves him lightly, then stares him down until he catches her meaning.

It used to be okay to joke about the llama farm or the spring-loaded poop flinger or fart recordings or any number of scandals that managed to make their way through every home in Raven Brooks after my summer adventures with Aaron, but not anymore.

"Sorry," Enzo says. "Didn't mean to bring up . . ."

I know they're trying to be nice, but I wish my friends would stop being so careful with me and just ask me about what it is they're afraid of making me remember. I mean, it's not like I've forgotten anything. It's not like I haven't been thinking about what happened to Aaron and Mya every second of every day since I found that note floating across the street from the broken window of Aaron's bedroom, the smear of blood that streaked across the paper, the way he tried to warn me against exactly what I'm doing now.

If my friends knew—if *anyone* knew—about the investigating I've been doing ever since I found that note, they wouldn't be avoiding the topic of Aaron and Mya. They'd be avoiding *me*.

"I want tacos," Trinity says, skipping over the awkward silence. "Who's in?"

"Can't. Gotta practice," Enzo says, slapping the basketball so it makes a hollow bonk, then shaking the sting off because he slapped it too hard.

"All I want is my bed," I say, already dreading the walk home. Seriously, can sleep deprivation kill you?

Trinity shrugs. "Didn't want to hang out with you two anyway."

Maritza strides ahead. "Later, dorks."

I start sweating again. What is wrong with me?

* * *

At home, I lie in bed with my eyes closed, but the sun is too bright and my clothes are uncomfortable and my parents are too loud downstairs even though it's the same chatter and laughter I always hear when they're making dinner.

"Get a grip," I say to my empty room, hoping my brain will listen and stop showing me reruns of last night, the horrible dream and the feel of the pale hand as it latched itself to my wrist.

It's no use, though. Whether my eyes are open or closed, no matter how much my bones ache from last night, the same reality remains. Aaron and Mya are missing, and no one but me seems to be bothered enough by it to do anything.

I try to get out of dinner by saying I don't feel well, but after Mom feels my forehead and says she's not buying it, I decide to go with an alternate plan: Get in and out of dinner as fast as possible.

Most normal kids have normal parents who ask them normal questions when they get home from school, questions like "How was your day?" or "Did you make any new friends?" Ever since we moved to Raven Brooks, though, my parents are never home when I get home, so they interrogate me over beef-stuffed peppers and three-bean salad.

And because we are far from normal, the conversation goes more like this:

CUT TO:

INT. 909 FRIENDLY COURT—NIGHT

The ROTH FAMILY—NICKY ROTH (12), awkward as humanly possible; LUANNE ROTH (41), smartest mom on the planet; and JAY ROTH (42), journalist with a love of educational music and Hostess® products—sits down to dinner.

> **LUANNE**
> Tell me what your favorite subject was today.

> **NICKY**
> Um, social studies?

> **LUANNE**
> Is that a question?

NICKY

It was social studies.

LUANNE

(cutting through her bell pepper)

Oh, how nice! Why was social studies your favorite today?

NICKY

(trying to find a way to make three-bean salad less disgusting)

I guess it was the . . . the thing about bills.

JAY

Could you be perhaps a bit more specific?

NICKY

The *lesson* about bills.

JAY

Right, so bills, as in, the documents that become laws?

NICKY

Yes, bills and laws.

LUANNE

Nicky, do I need to drag out the wheel?

NICKY

(remembering the "game" LUANNE crafted from the spinner she stole from the old Twister box and covered with masking tape labels like *How?* and *Why?* and *Tell me more!* to make talking about school seem like fun)

No! Don't get the wheel. The lesson
was about how bills are written, and
who writes them, and how they move
through, um, Congress and stuff to
become laws.

                    JAY
I'm just—

                LUANNE
Jay, don't.

                    JAY
Don't what?

                LUANNE
Don't sing the *Schoolhouse Rock!* song.

                    JAY
I wasn't going to. I was just going to
say that I knew a Bill.

LUANNE and NICKY stare intensely at JAY.

                    JAY
A Bill who lived on Capitol Hill.

                LUANNE
Jay.

                  NICKY
Dad.

                    JAY
Sorry.

                LUANNE
You know, your uncle Saul was a state
congressman.

Uncle Saul was without a doubt the most miserable person I've ever known. He had this deep groove that cut a path through the center of his forehead. My dad used to call it the Line of Disappointment. The only time the line faded was when he was watching baseball, but owing mostly to his devotion to the Chicago Cubs, baseball brought him misery more often than not, too.

JAY
Student council does look good
on a college application.

Recently, when they're not toiling over work or whether to replace the water heater, Mom and Dad seem to have decided that I have no real interests. They know I like to "tinker" with gadgets ("tinker" would be their word, not mine), but I suppose they think that twelve and a half is the perfect age for deciding on a career. Their suggestions are about as subtle as Mom's winks, which look more like convulsions.

After Mom has finished her stuffed pepper, and Dad and I have moved enough of it around on the plate to make it seem as though we've made a dent, Dad signals to me to clear the dishes, and he heads for the pantry. It's Twinkies tonight. He's been thinking about something.

So am I, so I grab two, and neither Dad nor my mom even flinch, which is how I know they're both distracted.

Mom starts, and it's immediately clear that this conversation has nothing to do with me.

"So, he's not backing off of it, huh?"

Dad shakes his head, looking down at his Twinkie. "Not even a little. It's that famous Esposito stubborn streak. It makes him a great managing editor, except—"

"Except when you don't agree with him," Mom finishes.

Okay, so using my highly attuned powers of deduction, I see they're talking about Dad's work, just like they have practically every night this week. Apparently, Enzo's dad wants my dad to go after a story he doesn't want to write, which is weird because they hardly ever disagree about stories. About anything, really.

"Maybe that means there's something there," Mom says, not meeting Dad's eyes.

"Oh, come on. Now you, too?" Dad says, and holy Aliens, he's lost interest in his Twinkie. Like, lost *all* interest. He turns in his chair to face my mom.

"Lu, the man just lost his wife. For all we know, he lost custody of his kids, too. If we're wrong, we're helping to ruin his life."

"Objectively speaking, you have to admit there are a lot of unanswered questions. I mean, it can't be coincidence that it's been three years since the guy's had a—"

"A job?" Dad says, and his face glows hot red.

"Hon, that's not what I meant."

"Because if we're going after people who can't hold a job down, we're in big trouble," Dad says, and Mom reaches for his hand.

"Jay, that's not how I meant it. I'm just saying he hasn't ever had to answer for some . . . incidents."

"I know you're talking about Mr. Peterson," I say.

At first, I thought they were tiptoeing around the conversation because I'm sitting right here, but when they turn to me with matching wide eyes, it's clear they've completely forgotten I was sitting here at all.

"He didn't lose custody," I say, and this is it. This is the moment I've been waiting for, when it's perfectly clear that my parents are willing to hear me. To *really* hear me about Mr. Peterson, about Aaron and Mya.

"Narf, I'm sorry," Dad says. "We shouldn't be talking about this in front of you. Miguel is your friend's dad. I don't want to put you two at odds."

"You have no idea," I mutter; Mom looks worried now.

"What do you mean?" she asks.

"It's just—look, that's not the point. The point is—"

"Are you boys having trouble? See, I knew it. I knew this was having an effect on him," Mom says, and it's like I'm not in the room again.

"Can we please tackle one crisis at a time?" Dad pleads, rediscovering his Twinkie and shoving it into his mouth absently.

"You guys aren't listening," I say, but I say it quietly because arguing with my parents isn't just futile, it's completely exhausting.

"Okay, then, how's this for a crisis?" Mom says, getting ready to launch. She leans toward my dad, who looks up at the ceiling, already signaling his surrender. "EarthPro is inches away from funding a new chemistry lab at the university. If Raven Brooks doesn't approve the purchase of the Golden Apple property, it'll be years before we can scrape together enough money."

"Well, then, problem solved!" Dad sighs, exasperated. "I'll just set aside my professional integrity in favor of your new lab."

"Well, dinner was delicious," I say, standing.

"And here I thought you were going to lecture me about Brenda Yi," Dad says to Mom.

"*Lecture* you? No, I have no intention of lecturing you, though seeing as it was her daughter who died, I'd say she deserves more than one vote in the matter, more than your friend across the street."

"My *friend*?" Dad laughs, but there's zero humor in his voice.

"And *dessert*," I say, patting my stomach, "was divine. Truly, Hostess® outdid themselves this time."

"I just don't understand where this brotherly love is

suddenly coming from," Mom says to my dad. "You barely even know the guy."

"You're right! And whose fault is that?"

"I don't recall saying it was a *bad* thing we didn't know him," Mom scowls.

"Really, I hate to go, but that homework isn't going to finish itself," I say, slinking up the stairs.

The last thing I hear is Mom saying something about Dad's bleeding heart and Dad saying something about Mom being as stubborn as her mother, and that's when I close my bedroom door.

I don't have any homework. I finished my life sciences quiz early, then did all my math problems and my sentence diagramming for English, then watched a fly bump against the window in the classroom trying to get out. Just as I started really feeling for the fly, the bell rang.

Dinners aren't usually that tense. It's this whole EarthPro thing—the fight over the land under the ruins of the Golden Apple empire. Up to this point, the land's been a sort of wound that never really healed over. Now all of a sudden, the bank wants to sell it, and everyone's scratching at the scab. If I had to guess, I'd say more than one set of parents was arguing over their stuffed peppers tonight, given the city council's announcement.

I make myself busy for the rest of the night: taking apart

and putting together an old receiver, then fine-tuning the focus on my binocuscope—an ingenious blend of binoculars and a periscope that I have intentions to patent one day. I even gather my dirty laundry from the corners of my room, pulling socks and shirts and underwear from behind my bookcase, next to my dresser, over my lampshade. When I sweep my hand under my bed, my knuckles scrape against something cold: a tin sign I've been avoiding for over three months, one that I can't work up the courage to unearth even now. And just like that, I'm back where I am every night.

I poke my head into the hallway to be sure my parents have called a truce for tonight. Once I hear snoring, I switch on my desk lamp and pull out my binder, finding

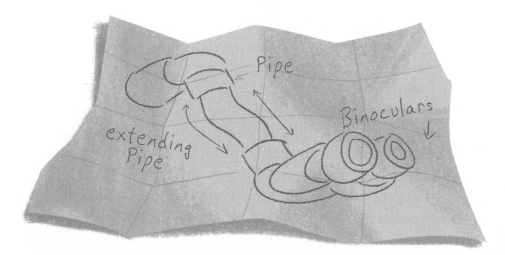

an odd comfort in the crinkled paper clippings and color-coded patterns. As my eyelids finally start to droop and my vision gets fuzzy with exhaustion, I drag myself back to bed, this time confident I'll be able to sleep, if for no other reason than a body can only stay awake for so long before collapsing.

As I drift off, I fight the nagging voice that tells me there's a thin line between dedication and obsession.

My last waking thought for the night is of Mr. Peterson, of his strange mind and disturbing behavior, and whether or not, before he got that way, he found comfort in something like a color-coded binder full of theories only he cares about.

Chapter 3

Dad's shoes tap loudly on the hallway floor as he paces. He always paces when he's trying to tie a bow tie.

"Over, then under and through, or over, through . . . Lu, is it under, then through, or over—?"

"Over, under, through!" Mom calls from the bathroom.

He sounds nervous. Actually, Mom sounds nervous, too. I can hear the clatter of her makeup brushes as she drops one and picks up another. The university has already had one fund-raising gala this year, and neither Mom nor Dad was this tense about that one, but the stakes are higher this time. Apparently, some bigwig from EarthPro is going to be there, and everyone's trying to impress her. Like if she likes the big party they're throwing, she'll just hand them a bucket of money to build their new chemistry lab.

"Seven fifteen," Dad warns.

"Well, I could go barefoot, but my colleagues might have some questions."

"Those shoes look fine."

"They make me look short."

"You *are* short."

"*You're* short!"

I peer through the crack in my bedroom door, and finally, there's the snickering I've been waiting for. Mom covers her mouth, but it's too late because Dad already saw her laughing, and now neither of them can be mad anymore.

Mom throws her hands up in defeat and heads downstairs to the car.

Dad is about to follow her but sees me watching from my room.

"We're abandoning you, but only for a few hours. Unless your mom starts in with her jokes, in which case, it could be longer."

He looks at me more seriously now, and I hate it when he does that because I know he's worried, more now than he was before we moved to Raven Brooks over the summer, more than he was every other time we moved. He thinks he knows how much this Aaron-and-Mya thing's been bothering me. He doesn't know the half of it.

"We don't have to go," he says, and I think part of him is looking for an excuse to stay home.

"I'm fine."

"Narf, your mom's worried. She isn't going to tell you that because she wants to be the cool parent, but she's worried," he says, but then he gives himself away. "I know you've been . . . watching. Across the street."

"I haven't—"

Dad puts up his hands in defense. "It's okay," he says, then checks himself. "Well, it's not okay. It's invasive and a little creepy, but I think I understand why. Nobody blames you for missing your friend."

Heat runs under my collar and up my neck as I try to understand how Dad has figured me out. There's no way he found my binder. It's not like Dad to go through my things. Besides, who looks for a false bottom in a twelve-year-old's desk drawer?

"Relax, Narf," he says, and he has no idea the feat he's asking me to achieve. "I'm not going to confiscate your binoculars."

The heat under my collar begins to cool as I slowly understand that he found my binocuscope.

"It's more than just binoculars, actually," I say.

"I'd expect nothing less," he says, and I might even detect a tinge of pride in his voice. "Anyway, you can keep it," he says, tugging on his bow tie hard enough to make it crooked. "Just stop using it to spy on the neighbors," he says. "Even Mr. Peterson. Promise?"

I nod so I don't have to lie, and he's out the door with a ruffle of my hair and a warning to go to bed at a decent hour.

Which tells me they won't be home until much later.

I wait until I see their taillights disappear around the corner, then wait a little longer just to be safe.

* * *

Even after the incident at Mrs. Tillman's store—even before Aaron went missing—Mom and Dad never expressly *forbade* me from going to the Golden Apple factory or the amusement park. Granted, that's probably because they never knew I'd been going to either of those spots in the first place, but still, I'm a rule follower at heart, even if only in the most literal sense.

They never said I couldn't go. So technically, it's not off-limits.

Not that I've wanted to go to the factory after finding the *Tooth 3* video. I still haven't been able to erase the memory of the Petersons on that tape, the way Aaron's dad so quickly became a different person, but one his family already knew. The twisted stranger in their father's skin.

Lately, though, something's been calling me back there. Maybe it's my curiosity about where Mr. Peterson goes when he leaves the house, the suspicion that he's revisiting old territory for reasons only people with a screw loose might understand. Or maybe there's still a shred of hope in me that imagines I'll see Aaron sitting there in the Office, rummaging through the filing cabinet for snacks, or Mya sitting in the park on the rusted-out carousel, waiting for me to figure out what she wanted from me that night last summer.

As I emerge from the overgrown brush that's begun to encroach on the wooded path leading to the train tracks, I see something I shouldn't see encircling the Golden Apple factory: a chain-link fence.

I come around the corner like I've never seen a fence before.

"Where did you come from?" I ask it, and I swear to the Aliens I half expect it to answer me because it wouldn't be that much weirder than this place—Aaron's place—being totally inaccessible now.

I run my eyes to the top of the fence and see coils of jagged razor wire strung along the ridge, a yellow sign with red lettering posted at eye level every several yards that warns me to KEEP OUT, a little picture of a stick figure trying to climb the fence with a big black X through the graphic, just in case the warning wasn't clear enough. The writing below the picture is small but no less authoritative.

KEEP OUT

PROPERTY OF RAVEN BROOKS
MUNICIPAL BANK AND TRUST.
TRESPASSERS WILL BE PROSECUTED.

Suddenly, it's like I haven't set foot on the grounds in years.

Suddenly, it's like a century since Aaron and Mya disappeared.

A raw layer of guilt exposes itself to the night air. I stare at the picture of the little Xed-out man and know all over again that I've let Aaron down.

How hard could it really be to find me? I can hear him ask. *Unless it's easier to forget me, like Enzo did.*

Guilt makes me brave for half a second, and I start pondering ways to climb over the fencing. Not because I want to get in, more to remind the fence and the little Xed-out man and the fine people of the Raven Brooks Municipal Bank and Trust whose factory this was before they decided to declare it theirs.

Then I spy an almost-hidden blinking red light at the corner of the fence where two circles of razor wire meet. A round eye follows my movements with mechanical precision. I imagine explaining the security camera footage to my parents, my second explanation in the company of a police officer within six months. Then I admit defeat, but not before punishing myself just a little more by imagining EarthPro looting the factory with all its picked locks and conveyer belt and filing cabinets full of snacks, its workers laughing over all the things that were important to the stupid kids who squatted here before the grown-ups finally got involved.

And maybe if I'd come by sooner, I could have salvaged some of it before it wasn't ours anymore.

I let all the guilt and shame and anger wash over me, blinding me to the overgrowth and the train tracks I stumble through as I make my way along the fence line. I've been walking ten minutes before I realize I've been going in the wrong direction. There's a reason I tripped over the train tracks—I zigged when I should have zagged. The wooded path leading home is behind me. I'm at the border of the amusement park again.

"Careful, Narf," I warn myself. "First sign of losing your marbles is aimless wandering."

I pause, then add, "Second sign is talking to yourself."

If it's possible, this side of the woods that surround the park is even more overgrown than the opposite side. I step through a tangle of shrubs only to drag my shin across a thorny blackberry vine, its sticky tentacles digging needle-thin scratches right through my jeans.

I hardly notice the pain, though, because ahead of me is a beige sort of tarp where one shouldn't be: strung between two tree trunks, mostly hidden from view by some overgrown brush, a flap of fabric hanging motionless on the still air.

I stop cold, flickers of every horror movie I've ever seen projecting in my mind. It could be anyone behind that tarp. A crazy hermit locked out of the factory where he used to seek shelter. A down-on-his-luck drifter with a grudge against twelve-year-old nerds.

A maniacal, single-toothed butcher bent on random carnage.

I begin to pivot on the same foot tangled in the black-berry vine, when a lone breeze ripples the canvas flap, lifting it just enough to spy some of the tent's contents. There's no cloaked menace or otherworldly monster lurk-ing beyond the covering. Just . . . papers.

I free my foot from its trap and edge toward the tarp, lifting the canvas and ducking under the opening that up close is clearly meant to be a door of some kind.

I don't know why I didn't bother to bring a flashlight. Maybe because I was so confident that I would be able to find my way to the factory. I squint through the inky night to pull into focus exactly what I'm looking at.

And it appears that I'm looking at some of the most incredible drawings I've ever seen.

I wouldn't call them beautiful. They're dark and unsettling, with more shadow than light, pen and charcoal smudges that blur the corners of the pages. There must be close to a hundred drawn on torn sheets of butcher-block paper, each a different carnival ride, strangely oversized and twisty, with curves too sharp to exist in real life and climbs that exceed the cloud line. One drawing depicts a Ferris wheel of epic proportions, the ride itself comprising a portion of a larger machine that

looks like the inner workings of a clock. Another imagines a carousel filled with live animals, leashed to their poles, lunging and rearing up and swiping. Another shows a roller coaster with a track spiraling straight up, its coils forming something akin to a DNA strand.

Almost as an afterthought, there are tiny people drawn into the landscape, so diminutive against the hulking rides that they may as well not exist at all.

Once I see those little people, though, I can't look away. It's only when I'm inches away from the butcher-block paper that I see their finely drawn expressions. Every person's face is drawn in terror, with lines creasing their eyes and foreheads and mouths. Their hands are traced into fists at their sides. Their legs are bent and buckling.

What could be a fairy-tale scene of fantasy rides that are larger than life is instead a full landscape of fear.

I walk around the tarp taking in the scene the artist has created, and my toe kicks a little box of pencils and a sharpener. Beside the box are a reusable water bottle, a small portable radio, a half-eaten pack of crackers, and a box of more butcher-block paper.

It's a makeshift artist studio.

"Whose, though?" I breathe, unable to tear my eyes from the dizzying scene protected in this fort. These drawings remind me of some that I've seen before, but the detail in the faces . . .

Quietly at first, then a little louder, I start to hear a soft tapping against the canopy above me, and when I look up, I see darkened spots on the canvas telling me it's begun to rain.

I'm reluctant to leave, but the rainstorms here don't seem to blow over quickly. They might come on fast, but they stay for a while.

Right on cue, a flash of lightning suddenly lights the fort, bringing the landscape to life for a second before a rumble of thunder shakes the air.

I take a deep breath and prepare to trek home, when another flicker of lightning casts a shadow against the back of the tarp I didn't see the last time—the unmistakable figure of a person.

Thunder rolls again and this would be the perfect opportunity to run, but I'm paralyzed.

Another flash of lightning, and again, the looming figure of a person standing inches from the back of the tarp towers over me.

Run! What is wrong with you? Run!

A third flash of lightning follows the last ripple of thunder, and this time I realize that the figure against the tarp hasn't moved. If this really is someone's shelter, why are they just waiting for me to leave?

I finally remember how to make my feet move and emerge carefully from under the tarp, using the flashes of lightning to light my way to the back of the fort. Fortunately, the storm is loud enough to drown the voice that's screaming at me that this is a horrible idea.

Just as I round the corner to the back of the shelter, a crack of thunder rips through the sky, and instead of jumping backward, I accidentally leap forward, straight into a cold, looming form.

The storm swallows my scream, but through flashes of lightning, I begin to piece together the picture.

A long body with jointed arms. No legs, but a pole that joins to four small wheels. A head with no face. A horrifying robotic mannequin looming over me.

And there's one more thing, a detail I missed at first glance, but one that finally convinces me to run: The hands at the ends of those jointed arms are bound behind the mannequin by a thick ring of electrical tape.

As I scramble out of the fort, blackberry vines snag and pull at my pant leg, but I drag myself free, swatting away reaching branches. I trip twice over bulging tree roots, but I hardly feel the impact of the ground. The faster I run, the harder the rain pounds against my face. My lungs burn and my legs shake, but I keep running, gaining speed and losing courage.

I've made my way through the woods and back to the asphalt streets of suburbia, but I barely notice. It's not until I skid past the street sign marking Friendly Court that I allow my pace to slow. By the time I reach my own porch, I can hear the high wheeze of my breath over the dying storm. Inside my house, silence sits heavy on top of the air.

"Mom? Dad?"

The house is still dark, though. They aren't home yet. I check the clock and see that it's not even ten. I was gone for little over two hours.

I shower to try to calm myself down, allowing the steam to ease my breathing and the soap to clean out the scrapes on my shins. I try so hard not to ask myself whose studio that was, why everyone was so scared, what the mannequin was. I want to believe it was nothing.

But as I pull the sheets over my head and try to focus on the ticking of the clock and the promise of Mom and Dad coming home soon, I can't scratch away the lines on the faces of those tiny people in the drawings, the looming figure of a bound mannequin, and the strange familiarity of the entire scene.

Because I'd swear I've seen those horrible, twisty rides. I'd swear I've seen the jointed plastic of those mannequins. And though I can't pinpoint how, I know that whatever it is I found behind the old Golden Apple factory, it has something to do with Aaron and Mya.

Chapter 4

At first, I think I'm finally having a good dream. The sun is warm on my shoulders, and a soft breeze parts the hair at the back of my head. Everything about the day—the sun, the wind, the warmth—makes my scalp tingle. With my eyes closed, I imagine myself in the middle of a perfect summer afternoon.

Then I start to move. When I open my eyes, I'm looking down at my feet, and they're tucked into the shadows of whatever I'm sitting in.

What was a breeze a second ago whips into a wind, and suddenly the sun is too bright and the warmth is an uncomfortable, claustrophobic heat. I look up just in time to see smears of white clouds all around me. I look down, and I can't find the ground. I'm sitting on the hard metal of a shopping cart, and a thick bar locks my legs in place, pressing against my lap with a viselike grip.

I'm moving faster now, leaned backward at an incline. What I see in front of me makes my stomach twist: a steep, sloping set of tracks climbing higher and higher through the clouds. When at last I reach the top, I dare to turn around, and I find that I'm not alone in the car. There, with its empty face and bound hands, is the mannequin from last night, frozen in its seat, waiting for the same drop I'm waiting for.

I scream as the car tips forward, the metal bar barely keeping me in my seat as we plummet toward the ground, crashing through the clouds and skipping off the tracks. The skin of my face ripples against the force, and I hold the metal bar for dear life, encircling it with my arms. Suddenly, the bar releases, and my body whips upward, chasing gravity toward the ground as I struggle to hang on with one arm.

I can see the ground now, and it's coming fast, so fast that I look for ways to brace for impact, but there's nothing I can do. I can only wait for the fall. Maybe then this will end.

Maybe.

Except now I see the ground clearly, and there are more robot mannequins, flitting in and out of the shops and shelters that make up this nightmare amusement park. Their tiny wheels move their long bodies unsteadily, flinging limbs in every direction as they struggle to keep upright under the speed. As my car approaches the ground, they all look up, and my body whiplashes against the velocity.

Then the mannequin who shares my car turns its head slowly on its neck, and through the wind whistling in my ears and the buzzing of those strange figures below, I hear it: screaming. It's screaming, trying to open wide a mouth that does not exist.

* * *

I wake with a gasp, my throat burning. I squeeze the sides of my mattress until my fingers cramp, but I don't trust that I'm safe yet. My stomach is doing summersaults like I'm still falling.

But the sun is bright behind my curtains, a different bright than it was in my dream, and I can hear Dad's voice coming from somewhere downstairs, so I venture slowly out of bed.

I ache all over. The burning in my throat seems to have moved to the side of my waist, and I realize it's because I'm absently scratching at it. When I lift my shirt and twist, I see that I've apparently been clawing at the same spot on my skin all night. Red fingernail marks have scraped the area raw, and as I bend a little closer, I find a tiny thorn protruding from the seam on my shirt. I pluck it out and flick it away.

A splinter doesn't explain the grass stuck between my toes, though.

"What the—?"

The bottoms of my feet are dirty, and as I duck my head to examine them closer, a tiny leaf falls from my hair, floating to the floor.

I reluctantly think back to last night. The fort, the drawings of all the little people, the mannequin with its bound wrists. The reality was bad by itself, but the dream that followed is enough to make my hands start trembling all over again.

But the grass. The leaf. The splinter.

I showered last night.

I'm still scratching my side when I lumber down the stairs, and Dad's voice gets louder. He's on the phone.

"That's not what I'm saying. Miguel, listen to me, please. I never said that."

He's in his study at the end of the hallway, the dark little room with no window that I'd lobbied to make mine before Mom determined it would be a death trap if there was ever a fire. Dad was thrilled to have a little corner all to himself for the days he worked from home, and by the first night in our new turquoise house, I was secretly glad I'd lost that battle. Not only was the room dark, the hallway leading to it didn't have a light, either. It was like someone built the room specifically to scare the bejesus out of anyone wondering what was around the corner in that pitch-dark hallway.

This'll be where I bury the bodies, Dad had said upon winning the room. He loves old gangster movies. But I wondered if maybe he regretted the room after the first night, too, when he had to grab one of Mom's scented candles just to light his way to the office and click on the dim lamp on his desk.

He doesn't sound scared now, though. He sounds worked up. But also tired, if that's possible.

"Look, all I'm saying is that we need to consider the implications of running the story. People in this town are already starting to take sides."

I hear the crinkle of unwrapping plastic. It's got to be Ho Hos. It's not even eight in the morning, but Dad sounds pretty stressed. If he brought a Ho Ho into his office, he must have known his conversation with Mr. Esposito was going to be tense.

"I recognize that, but I also know that Brenda Yi is a close friend of yours, and—"

Dad sighs and makes a couple of attempts to interject, but as I creep down the hallway toward his study, I can hear the voice of Mr. Esposito on the other line. I don't need to hear him to know what he's saying.

"Of course we do, but we need to think of the other side, too!" Dad argues. "A pro-development bent is by default an anti-Peterson bias. The courts never faulted the guy. That deserves some investigation, too. Otherwise, we run the risk of dragging a man through the mud who's just lost his whole family!"

A fresh wave of nausea rolls over me. Mr. Peterson just lost his whole family. As though Aaron and Mya are already as lost as Mrs. Peterson.

Permanently lost.

"We'll talk when I get in," Dad says, and sets the phone down a little harder than necessary.

He's crinkling his wrapper when he rounds the corner of the hallway and runs straight into me.

"Man alive, Narf! If you're trying to scare me to death, you have next to no inheritance."

"Sorry," I say, for scaring . . . and for the argument.

Dad pats me on the shoulder. "Guess you heard all that."

I nod.

"Then I should be the one who's sorry," he says. "We're just, not seeing eye to eye. Professionally," he adds, like that makes it better somehow.

It's basically a rehashing of the argument he had with Mom the other night, only there's a new twist: I had no idea Mr. Esposito and Lucy Yi's mom were friends. Part of me wonders if they connected over their loss—Mrs. Yi losing her daughter, and Mr. Esposito losing his wife. Enzo and Maritza don't talk much about their mom, but from the few comments they have made, I know she died from cancer, and I know they were both too young to remember her. The family keeps a big, silver-framed picture of her on their mantel with some candles and fresh flowers. She was beautiful, with dark brown hair like Maritza's and a smile that I bet Mr. Esposito still thinks about.

All I know about Brenda Yi is that she's smart like my mom and a lawyer who pretty much never loses a

49

case. She does a lot with the Raven Brooks city council, and apparently, she's been working hard to get the Golden Apple Amusement Park leveled for a long time, something nobody knew about until the whole EarthPro debate started. I've heard Mrs. Tillman whispering a little too eagerly to customers at the natural grocer about Mr. Yi and how he was so devastated by the accident that he had a breakdown and moved to Canada, leaving his wife, the town of Raven Brooks, and every last memory of his daughter behind.

"Why does it matter if Mr. Esposito is friends with Mrs. Yi?" I ask my dad on our way to the kitchen.

Dad's quiet for a second while he pours himself some more coffee. "It *shouldn't* matter," he says pointedly.

"So, you think he only wants you to run a mean story about Mr. Peterson because he's on Mrs. Yi's side?"

Dad stares hard into his coffee cup, his forehead creased. "Well, when you put it like that, it doesn't seem so complicated," he says, then smiles a little.

"I don't think he's innocent," I say to Dad, and Dad's smile fades a little.

"See, the thing is, Narf, we should have something more than just suspicion before we write a story about the guy."

"So, you just need some proof," I say, staring down at my dirty feet, bits of grass making the spaces between my toes itch.

He takes a sip of his coffee and stares at me. "Did I ever tell you how I knew I wanted to be a journalist?"

I shake my head.

"When I was younger I was at the park with my buddies, and this family walks up to an old man, and he's holding a dog. This family starts walking toward the man and his dog, and all of a sudden, the little kid that was with the family calls out to the dog, and the dog goes running to him. Doesn't even look back at his owner, just goes straight to the kid. It's only after that happens that I notice the guy behind the family with a notepad, and another guy behind him with a camera. And the family all poses for a picture, and they ask the kids questions, and the guy with the notepad writes down their answers, and then they all leave."

"The old man and the dog leave with the family?" I ask.

"No, the family leaves with the dog and the reporter, and the old man stays behind."

"Hang on, they took his dog?"

Dad smiles one of those smiles that's too sad to be a real smile. "No, they took *their* dog. I read about it in the paper the next day. See, this family had lost their dog five years prior during a storm. Turns out, the dog was fine. He'd been living one county over with this widower who took him in during the storm."

"So . . . did the old guy get, like, visitation rights or something afterward?"

"I have no idea," Dad says.

"But I mean, he was a widower. And then he had this dog for five years, and then he just loses the dog, too?"

Dad shrugs, but he's watching me closely.

"Is this why we were never allowed to get a dog?" I ask.

Dad looks down, and in a tone he only uses after someone's died or he's apologizing to Mom, he says, "It's why I became a journalist. Because nobody asked the questions you just asked. Nobody told the old man's story."

I try to picture the sad life of this old man who lost so much. I think about my dad and all the things he's lost over the years: the newspapers he called work, the houses he called home.

"Here's the thing, Narf," he says. "Life can take almost everything away, but there are a few things you can hold on to. For me to be a good journalist—to be a good human being—I have to hold on to my integrity. Without that, I'm . . ."

"Lost," I say.

He nods. "It's not the press's job to decide who's right. It's our job to tell the stories. *All* the stories."

We're quiet for a minute while Dad sips his coffee.

Then I say, "I don't think you'd lose your integrity if you wrote a story about Mr. Peterson being a bad guy."

Dad's eyebrows scrunch together. "Narf, whatever you think you saw Mr. Peterson doing when you were playing Inspector Gadget up there, trust me, you saw nothing. The guy's a little weird, I'll give you that, but it's no reason to blame him for a horrible accident from years ago," Dad says, setting down his coffee cup. He looks so tired.

"That's not it," I say, pushing aside the Inspector Gadget comment. "I think there's more."

Dad eyes me warily.

"I-I'm not sure that Aaron . . ."

This is the moment when I tell him everything. I bring my binder downstairs and let Dad go through all of it. I answer every question he has, and I take him to the Golden Apple factory, and I take him past the old park and show him—

Show him what? What do I really have? I have a note from Aaron I can't explain. I have a pattern of behavior I can't comprehend. I have a treasure trove of strange drawings and a creepy mannequin and countless questions and zero answers. I have absolutely no reason for my dad to write a story that makes Mr. Peterson the bad guy, a story that would stop him from fighting with Mr. Esposito, that might just let him keep this job for more than six months, that could make Brenda Yi feel like someone actually cares that her daughter died and maybe, just maybe, that it was someone's fault.

And I have nothing that could convince my dad to walk me down to the police station and tell them that I don't believe for a second Aaron and Mya are at some aunt's house in another state.

"You're not sure that Aaron what?" Dad asks, looking more worried than ever, and why do he and Mom always seem to look at me like that lately?

I try to say something to make that worry melt from his face. A joke would be good now. Saying *anything at all* would be good. But I can't think of a single thing.

Just then, the phone rings. My dad watches me for three rings, hoping I'll tell him what I can't seem to, but after the fourth ring, he runs for the phone he left in his office.

"Right. Okay. Right, I'll be in shortly. It's fine, Miguel, I understand."

I hear him hang up, but I'm already upstairs, staring at my grass-stained feet and accepting the unacceptable: I must have walked somewhere in my sleep. I went digging again. It's the only explanation for the dirt under my nails, the grass, the splinter.

And while I want to believe it's because there's some subconscious drive to find that critical piece of evidence that will make my dad write the story he needs to write, I don't actually believe that's the reason my crazy brain is making me sleepwalk to the last place I'd ever want to go at night.

I think my crazy brain is trying to tell me that there's something else to find there.

Chapter 5

I t's parent-teacher night, which means Mom and Dad get to hear about how I show great potential but struggle to maintain focus on topics that don't interest me. I keep wondering what the magic age is when I can stop pretending to care about what year Alaska became a state and start learning about how to keep my night-vision lenses from fogging up when it's humid out. Anyway, I know I have a night of lectures about goals and homework habits ahead of me after Mom and Dad get home, so in a way, I deserve this trip to Golden Apple Amusement Park.

I keep forgetting how early it gets dark in the winter; I can already see my breath against the night, and it's only six o'clock. Leaves crunch under my feet, and even though I know exactly where I'm going, the path to the park looks eerie and unfamiliar now. Ever since I found the stash of sketches on the other side of the factory, it's almost like this path, these trees, this whole wooded area that expands all the way to the train tracks has been fooling me all along by making me think I knew it.

These woods aren't mine, though. They belong to the ghosts left behind by the Golden Apple Corporation.

"Eyes on the prize, Nicky," I say when I catch myself peering over my shoulder every few steps. "You're here for evidence."

These woods may not belong to me, but I seem to have made myself right at home in my sleep. After my talk with Dad, it's the only place I could think of that might hold some clue to where Aaron and Mya are, and what Mr. Peterson knows about it. If my sleeping brain wants to dig, then maybe it's time for my waking brain to do the same.

The Golden Apple Amusement Park has never been inviting, not since I first saw it. Even though the pictures of its grand opening, from the paper, showed it in its glory days, all I've ever seen when I've looked at it was the charred remnants of the front entrance and the angry graffiti covering whatever's left. Still, somehow the entrance to the park looks even less welcoming than it did this summer. Maybe it's the leafless trees that make every branch look like a crooked hand strangling the park, or the cold, glistening dew that makes the abandoned machinery look like it's breathing. Whatever it is, I've never disliked this place more.

"Get in and get out," I say, reminding myself I'm here for a reason.

I head straight for the last place I found myself in my dream—the back of the park.

But when I nudge past the last of the grasping branches, I'm startled to find someone else standing at the base of the Rotten Core.

"And here I was thinking I was the only kid who liked to hang out in the middle of abandoned amusement parks at night," I say. "Is this, like, a new cool thing to do?"

Maritza turns to me, looking either annoyed or relieved.

"No," she says. "You're not cool."

Annoyed. Definitely annoyed.

"Sorry," I say, fumbling for something to ease the tension. "Didn't mean to interrupt you . . ."

She shakes her head, and her face softens. "It's not your fault. I was just thinking."

I can't say anything else because I know what it's like to get lost in a memory here, too. And I don't have half the memories of this place that Maritza must have. Still, she doesn't ask me what I'm doing here, so she must know that I'm looking for answers, too.

Answers to questions I don't know how to ask.

Maritza glances back at me. "Do you really think they're staying with family?"

Clearly, Maritza knows how to ask those questions, though.

"What?"

She turns fully, squaring her shoulders to face me. To challenge me.

"Aaron and Mya. Do you really think they were sent to live with some relative in Minnesota?"

"I—I don't know about Minnesota," I say, not exactly answering the question. Why am I all of a sudden so afraid to talk about this?

Because you haven't talked about it yet.

In fact, I haven't said a word about it. I've lived the truth that I believe—that Maritza believes—for over three months now, but I haven't let myself breathe a single word of it out loud. Every suspicion is contained between the covers of my three-ring binder.

"So do you believe it?" she asks, but it sounds more like pleading. Maritza's round brown eyes and creased forehead want me to say the words I thought I've been wanting to say all this time.

Only now does it occur to me that maybe it's been a relief to *not* have to say it. Maybe to say it to someone else would make it too real—that Aaron and Mya aren't at some relative's house, hiding from the fresh tragedy of Raven Brooks. That maybe they're closer to the tragedy than anyone else is willing to admit.

"No," I say to Maritza. "No, I don't believe it."

She doesn't ask me anything more. It seems to be enough

that we agree on what we *don't* believe. There'll be time to talk about what we do believe later.

"It's hard to imagine this used to be the place that felt the safest," she says, gazing at the charred woods around us, the overgrowth rising through the ashes and winding around the equipment that remains, smeared in the oily residue left from the fires.

Safe isn't the first feeling that comes to mind.

"It was where we felt . . . I dunno. Understood," she says.

Maritza absently fiddles with the golden apple charm that dangles from the bracelet she's wearing. I recognize it immediately, and I brush away the chill that creeps through me as I remember my dream from the other night.

The golden bracelet I tried to unearth from the ash and soil.

The hand it was attached to.

The body that rose up from the dirt, its jerking arms, reaching out for me.

I look up, and Maritza follows my gaze.

"I think about Lucy all the time," she says, still playing with the charm around her wrist. "And Mya, too. I never talk about them anymore. I know you probably think I don't care, that I forgot about them, but I haven't."

Under the silver moonlight, I can see Maritza's eyes grow glassy with tears.

"I don't think that," I say.

I couldn't begin to know what Maritza has gone through—losing one friend at such a young age, only to be driven off in fear from another friend. I wonder if this is why Maritza has been hanging out with Enzo, Trinity, and me more all of a sudden, because she's been looking for someone to talk to about this as much as I have.

"It's cool that you all kept them," I say, nodding toward the bracelet Maritza doesn't seem to realize she's fiddling with.

She looks confused. "We didn't. At least, I don't think so. Mya never wore hers after the accident. She said the clasp broke, but I think she just didn't want to be reminded."

She looks up at the tree. "They never found Lucy's."

Just then, we hear a distant rustling at the other end of the park, the end that was once the entrance. The sound of rustling bushes turns to the unmistakable sound of heavy footfalls.

Without a word, Maritza and I run into the tangle of overgrowth webbed between the trees and peer through the leaves, taking turns breathing.

The rustling grows louder until a familiar figure breaks through the brush.

With his eyes wide and focused and his tightly curled mustache waxed to fine points, Mr. Peterson appears in the clearing armed with a large wheelbarrow better suited for transporting mulch than . . . whatever he's planning to transport from an abandoned amusement park under cover of darkness.

I venture a look at Maritza, but her eyes are trained on Mr. Peterson.

He looks over his shoulder, then slowly at the panorama of trees and bushes around him before lifting the wheelbarrow's handles and pushing it to the other side of the Rotten Core.

"Go!" Maritza hisses, but I put a hand up and point to the landscape on that side of the roller coaster. Hardly a single leaf clings to the branches in that section of the woods. Going in for a closer look would leave us exposed.

"I can't see anything," Maritza whispers, teetering on tiptoe to squint above the bushes that cover us.

"I know. I can't, either. But we can't—"

I don't have a chance to finish my sentence before Maritza is on the move, hunkered low as she picks her way through the brush.

"Maritza!" I whisper, but it's no use. Either she can't hear me or she's ignoring me. My choices are to stay where it's safe or—

"This is a horrible idea." I sigh, crouching low like she does, but she's smaller and more coordinated, so she somehow avoids catching her clothes on the protruding branches and rattling the trees as she moves.

We've made it halfway to the other side of the roller coaster when we run out of cover, but it's still a better vantage point than we had before.

Mr. Peterson is rummaging around in what looks like a black box at first. Soon, though, I realize it's the soot-stained carcass of a roller coaster car. As he bangs around in the metal drum, all I can see are his elbows while he grunts and grumbles, occasionally cursing under his breath.

Maritza shifts beside me. "What's he . . . ?"

With one last curse, he yanks out a series of wires from the innards of the old roller coaster car.

"Why would there be wires in there?" I breathe.

This time it's Maritza's turn not to answer.

After dumping the wiring into the wheelbarrow, he looks up like he's just remembered something, then mutters, "In the . . . the fun house. Right, the fun house."

Then, still mumbling under his breath, he disappears through the overgrowth toward the entrance of the park, leaving Maritza and me without even a question to ask each other this time.

He emerges from the dark as quickly as he left, a multi-colored plastic platform full of chips and circuits clutched in one hand. A motherboard.

Mr. Peterson starts muttering again, this time a little louder, silver puffs of air trailing the end of each word.

"Just need a processor for the . . . then a splitter to . . . no, no, no, no, that won't work because—shhhh, stop talking, just stop *talking*!"

He's pacing now, squeezing the motherboard in one hand and pressing his other hand to the side of his head.

"I can fix it. I can fix it. I just need . . . *no!*"

Maritza takes a step backward, and so do I, but the dead trees form jail bars all around us. Everywhere I turn, there's another branch picking at the sleeve of my jacket, another twig underfoot.

Then Mr. Peterson stops, his hands dropping to his knees, his mutterings turning to sobs. "Why won't it stop?" he gasps, letting go of his knees and covering his head like he needs to protect it. Then, with some strange, dawning clarity, he tilts his head to the night sky and bellows, "What have you done?"

Maritza shoots her hand to my arm, grasping it so tight her fingernails dig into my skin. If I'd been expecting it, I wouldn't have shouted.

But I wasn't.

Maritza gasps, and her hand flies to my mouth. Then my hand covers her mouth, but it's too late.

Mr. Peterson doesn't move. His head is still raised to the moon, his hands still pressed against his cheeks. He waits like we wait. Then, with excruciating slowness, he levels his head and lowers his arms to his side. He looks straight ahead at first, then turns in our direction.

Tiny wisps of silver breath are escaping through the spaces in our fingers, but we don't dare uncover our mouths.

Leaves still cover us. From this distance in the dark, it's nearly impossible that he could actually see us. Yet he looks straight at us anyway, almost as though he knew we were there all along.

"Children?" Mr. Peterson whispers in a voice that might sound playful from a sane person, not a person looting an amusement park and screaming at the moon.

"Children, come play. Come play."

Maritza makes a sound from behind my hand, or maybe that was me.

Mr. Peterson starts to laugh, a low rumble that sounds like it starts from his toes before it gains speed and burbles out of his mouth. He's still looking straight through the leaves in our direction. His eyes are wide and wild, and his mustache is curled high enough to reach his eyebrows.

"Come play, children!" he screams between maniacal giggling, and Maritza snaps me from my trance, practically yanking my arm from its socket as she pulls me toward thicker brush and through the old park entrance until we reach the path leading back toward my neighborhood.

We take turns looking behind, unable to hear past our own thundering feet. We run until my legs give out, and I have to sit on the curb while they turn to jelly. There's a curb to sit on, though, which means we're out of the woods.

Maritza stands over me, panting but otherwise fine, like maybe she could have run another sprint away from the loony tune who lives across the street from me. I look up at the green sign marking our place and see that we've completely overshot Friendly Court and wound up closer to Maritza's.

"We're okay," she says between swallows while she works to steady her breathing. "I don't think he followed us."

We walk on shaking legs (okay, I walk on shaking legs) the remaining two blocks to Maritza's house without a word. First, she tried to say something, then I tried to say something, and then we both gave up. Only when we're standing on her driveway does she say, "That happened, right?"

"Yeah, that happened," I say.

"Well, at least you saw it, too," she says, and suddenly, for the first time since Aaron went missing, I don't feel alone. Something about the way Maritza's eyes scan my face makes me think she feels the same way, and it occurs to me that she's the only other person outside of the Peterson family that's witnessed a hint of the strangeness I have. She had that one encounter with Mr. Peterson, too, right after Lucy died, and it was enough to keep her from coming back to that house.

"I saw it, too," I say, just because it feels like we need to say it to make it real.

"Hey, should you go get your brother?" I say. "He should know what happened."

Maritza shakes her head. "He'll . . . be kind of mad when he finds out I was in the park. He doesn't know that I go there sometimes. Maybe you can talk to him about it tomorrow? I'll fill in Trinity."

I wait until she goes inside and locks her door before I walk away, my heart revving up its engine again because what if Mr. Peterson did follow us out of the woods? What if he's watching from the darkness?

I take the longer way home because it's farther from the entrance to the woods. I cut through the yards without dogs until I reach Friendly Court and have no choice but to head in the direction of my house . . . and the Petersons'.

Just then, I see a pair of headlights turn the corner, and my heart stops beating for a moment while I wait to see which driveway they pull into. When I see the car turn into mine, I run the rest of the way to meet my parents.

"Hey, Narf! Fancy meeting you here," Dad says as he opens the passenger side door. My mom is the first to notice, as always, that something looks wrong.

"Why are you sweating?" she asks.

"Oh, you know. Just out for a jog," I say.

"A jog?" she asks, looking concerned. "Are you bleeding?"

I look down at my hand to find angry scratches from

the branches I swatted aside during my sprint through the woods.

"Did you get into a fight, Nicky?" Mom asks, worry crinkling her entire face. Oh, if only I'd been in a fight. It would have been so much easier.

"Nah, just cut it on the . . . uh, the trellis," I say, remembering the rotting wood on the slatted board outside of my window.

Mom raises an eyebrow, then looks at Dad.

"Don't look at me. I didn't sic the trellis on him," Dad says, but it's becoming clear that my nighttime adventures are at risk of exposure.

"How was parent-teacher night?" I ask, eyeing Mr. Peterson's house while I coax my parents inside.

"Great," Dad says. "Apparently, you're an unmotivated genius."

"The good news is, I have a plan for that," Mom says.

"Oh yeah?" I say, not hearing a word of the conversation. All I can do is focus on getting inside the house before Mr. Peterson returns.

"Yep. I'm going to need to repurpose the conversation wheel, but it'll be worth the sacrifice," Mom says, but "sacrifice" just makes me think of human sacrifice, and is that what Mr. Peterson's doing? Oh, holy Aliens, is he sacrificing children to appease some kind of amusement park god?

"Can we go inside?" I plead.

"You know, Lu, we could just buy a new Twister game for the spinner. I'd hate to see you dismantle the conversation wheel. You worked so hard on that."

"You know me so well," Mom coos.

Or maybe it's not just kids. Maybe Mr. Peterson is sacrificing happy people. Maybe he's so profoundly unhappy that he's searching out anyone with a trace of happiness and snuffing them out one by one. Aaron *was* having more fun this past summer than he had been before . . . I think.

"Can we please just go through the door?"

"You know, I kind of like that spinner from the Life game. Remember how it had that satisfying *click click click* every time you'd turn the wheel?" Mom says.

"Oh yeah, that was a good spinner," Dad agrees.

"Are you serious right now? Inside, people! Inside!" I yell, and my mom's palm flies to my forehead.

"Are you coming down with something?"

"If I say yes, can we go inside?" I beg, running out of options.

"Fine, but tomorrow, we spin for goals," she says, guiding me inside.

"It's like bowling for dollars, but without the fun or the money," Dad says.

At this point, I'd be willing to cross-stitch for crocodiles if it meant getting off this driveway and going into the house.

Upstairs, I pretend to go straight to bed, but instead I go straight to my window. I watch for Mr. Peterson's headlights until I can't keep my eyes open anymore. I want to call Maritza, but I'm afraid Mr. Esposito would answer, and then I'd have to explain to him why I'm calling his daughter at nine o'clock at night.

Finally, I curl up on top of my covers without even changing into my pajamas, trying but failing to block the sound of Mr. Peterson's unhinged laughter.

Chapter 6

The entire day feels like it's dragged on for a year, and eighth period was especially painful with Ms. Collier droning on about the difference between an equilateral triangle and an isosceles.

"I mean, have you ever—I mean, *ever*—looked at a triangle and been like, 'You know, it's nice, but it would be so much better if it were equal on all sides'?" Enzo says, and I want to laugh, but I barely slept last night, and he keeps trying to dribble his basketball, but he only manages to dribble it for a second before kicking it. Then he has to chase it and start all over again.

If he would just stop for a second, I could tell him about what happened last night. That is, if Maritza hasn't already, which I doubt or otherwise he wouldn't be trying out his jokes about triangles.

"We have to tell someone," Trinity says, appearing out of thin air somewhere behind Enzo. Maritza's beside her a second later.

"I told her everything in PE," Maritza says to me. Then, as further explanation, "It was square dance day."

We all nod. Everyone but Enzo.

"Told who everything? What's everything?"

Trinity and Maritza look at me like I've failed them.

"You haven't told him yet?" Maritza accuses.

"I haven't had a chance. Anyway, aren't you the one who lives with him?"

"Would someone please tell me what I'm supposed to know?" Enzo says, holding the basketball against his stomach.

"It's kinda hard to explain," I say, fumbling for a place to start.

"No, it's not," Maritza says, and then turns to Enzo. "Mr. Peterson is a creeper. We're worried about Aaron and Mya. Nicky has proof."

"Huh?" Enzo says, and now all three of them are looking at me.

"Well, I'm not sure I'd call it *proof* exactly," I say.

Maritza rolls her eyes. "Okay, whatever, but we both saw him looking way suspicious last night."

"Wait, you two were together last night?" Enzo says, turning a furious eye to me.

"Not like that," Maritza says, and I think I say something along those lines, too, but honestly, I have zero idea of what I'm saying right now because I'm so tired, and my head is spinning, and I just need a second to get my thoughts together.

Maritza isn't having any of that, though.

"We need to do something. Mya and Aaron could be in trouble right now," she says, pulling on Enzo's arm like she wants him to actually walk over to Mr. Peterson's house right now, knock on his door, and demand to see his kids.

"Hang on," Trinity says, and like usual, we all stop and listen because let's be real, Trinity is the smartest one of all of us. "We all want to help Aaron and Mya, but we need more information first."

"But Nicky and I saw him last night!" Maritza pleads, and this piques Enzo's interest again.

"Yeah, go back to that. What did you and Nicky see, exactly?"

"She was just there!" I say defensively, and Maritza huffs a huge sigh.

"I was at the park."

"Why were you there? How late was it? Does Dad know?"

"Enzo." Trinity tries putting a hand on his arm.

"I just go there sometimes, okay? It's no big deal," Maritza says, suddenly quiet, and now we all are.

"She likes to go when she's . . . you know . . . missing Lucy and Mya," Trinity says to Enzo so quietly, I barely hear her, but Enzo's face softens, and he looks at me like

maybe he understands it's the same for me, when I'm missing Aaron.

"Okay, so what did you see?" Enzo asks, calmer now.

Then we all struggle, and it's Trinity who rescues us
again. "He was just . . . taking stuff. And looking for
something, I guess."

Maritza and I both nod, but Enzo looks from Maritza
to me and back to Maritza, and it's obvious he's waiting
for more.

"And he was, like, all agitated," Maritza says.

"Sooo, you saw him in the park, and you saw him taking some stuff," Enzo says, his eyebrows knitted. "Wow,
you're right. He's clearly some sort of evil genius."

"Ugh, *manito*, this is serious!"

"Of course, of course. You're obviously getting ready to
blow the top off this case."

"Nicky, tell him!" Maritza says, her eyes brimming with
hope, and just when I think I have nothing more to offer as
evidence to convince Enzo, I remember my binder.

"There's more," I say, but just as I open my mouth to
fully confess my suspicions, someone yells from across
the quad.

"Hey, Espozitti!"

The four of us turn to see Seth and Ruben, then look
around to see who they're talking to.

Enzo finally answers. "Hey!"

"You coming to practice or what?" Ruben says, and Seth turns toward the gym, already bored.

"Who's Espozitti?" Maritza asks.

"Isn't that a type of pasta?" Trinity asks.

"Um, yeah, I'm coming," Enzo says.

"Wait," Maritza says, betrayal all over her face. "You're leaving?"

Enzo looks at her like she's the crazy one. "I've got practice. By the way, Nicky, are you coming? Tryouts are soon—"

"But didn't you hear anything we just said?" she says, and suddenly I'm winded because the look on Maritza's face is exactly like the look on Mya's face that night in the park when I let her down, the moment I didn't know how to help her when it was most important.

"I heard you say that Mr. Peterson is weird, Maritza," Enzo says, then looks over his shoulder to make sure Ruben hasn't left without him.

"But—"

"*Manita*, chill, okay? It's probably nothing. You're letting your imagination run wild," Enzo says, his voice softening, but he's already backing away from us and toward Seth. "Nicky, you coming?"

I turn back to Enzo, and it's possibly the worst time to say this, but the words are fleeing my mouth in a frustrated stream before I can contain them. "Enzo, I'm not going to try out. It's not my thing, and this is more important."

I open my mouth to say more, but it's too late. Enzo has turned, and now he's running toward Seth, dribble-kicking the ball and stumbling to keep up. Their heads, shiny and gel-crunchy, disappear behind the gym door without a single glance back.

We're all silent while Maritza fumes and Trinity mumbles something and I try to erase the image of Mya's face that's seared itself onto my brain.

Finally, Trinity says, "Now what?"

I take a slow, deep breath. "Now we go to my house." I've already started walking when I say, "I have something to show you."

* * *

Trinity and Maritza turn the last page of the binder and stare at it for a minute. They haven't said a word the entire time they've been leafing through all my findings, and the wait has been pure agony. Just when I think they're finally about to say something, Maritza flips the pages over and starts at the beginning.

I can't take it anymore.

"You think I'm crazy," I say. I don't even bother to ask.

They look over their shoulders at me. As always, Maritza is the first one to talk.

"Oh yeah, you're crazy for sure," she says. "This is . . . detailed, Nicky."

"You practically have a record of everything he eats, when he sleeps, when he's awake," Trinity adds, and I can't be sure, but she looks a little afraid of me.

"I wouldn't be surprised if you said you had DNA samples from him, too," Maritza says.

I'm starting to regret sharing any of this with them, but I'm also starting to regret not collecting any DNA samples from Mr. Peterson, too, so I know they have a point.

"But," Trinity says gently, "you're not wrong."

Maritza nods. "It's weird. He goes out at night a lot, and when he does, he's gone for hours at a time."

"And these notes here about the sounds you've been hearing," Trinity says, flipping between my pages of notes. "Drilling, the music, screams. I have no idea what that is, but it's . . . I don't know, bizarre."

"Plus, the stuff you've found in the garbage, the meals for two!" Maritza says, and now they're both getting animated.

"Oh, right! I forgot about that!" Trinity says.

"So, you believe me?" I ask, daring to hope for the first time that I might not have to shoulder the burden of my creepy neighbor alone.

"For sure," Trinity says, and my relief is complete, but short-lived, because her eyes fall to the floor, and Maritza looks at her with the same doubt, and there it goes, all my hope.

"What?" I ask, not sure I want to know.

"*We* believe you," Maritza says.

"But we need more," Trinity finishes.

"What are you talking about?" I plead with them, grabbing my binder and flapping it around like a pair of wings. "I've got an entire book of evidence right here. Not to mention what we saw last night in the park!" I say.

"But what did we actually see?" Maritza asks, and I can't deny she's right. We have no idea what he was doing.

"And the food," she continues. "The dude could just be hungry."

"Those noises coming from the basement could be anything, too," Trinity says cautiously. "My grandpa used to build whole boats in his basement. Nicky, haven't you ever heard of circumstantial evidence?"

Honestly, I can't believe *she's* heard of circumstantial evidence.

"I watch *Law & Order*," she says, and that seems to be enough to convince us.

"Okay, okay," I say. "I get it. Weird, not criminal."

"And nothing here really says anything about Aaron and Mya. I mean, for all we know, they really did get shipped off to Minnesota, and this is just a book full of evidence that Mr. Peterson's last shred of sanity went with them," says Trinity.

But there's something they haven't seen yet, something I didn't dare to keep in the book.

I push past them and dig around at the bottom of my fake drawer, my fingers rattling the bracelet around until I pull it out by an end, letting the charm dangle in the light of my desk lamp while Maritza and Trinity follow it like a pendulum.

Maritza reaches for it slowly, and I can see her hand trembling in the waning light of my room.

"There's a chip in it," she says quietly, and Trinity's eyebrows gather in confusion. "Lucy's bracelet had a little chip in the apple. It almost looked like someone had taken a bite out of it. That's what we used to say."

She looks sick for a moment before a tear escapes down her cheek.

I freeze, realizing that the bracelet I'd been thinking this whole time was Mya's is actually Lucy's. My brain won't stop trying to understand what it means.

Maritza looks at me like she's forgotten I was even here. "How did you get this?"

If I didn't know better, I would almost think she was accusing me of stealing it. Trinity still looks confused, but I need to clear this part up first.

"Someone left it for me, in the trellis outside my window."

I watch Maritza to see if she's catching on.

"Before Aaron and Mya went missing," I say, and now both of them look lost.

"I think Mya left it for me," I say. "I thought it was hers."

"I still don't understand," Maritza says. "How did she have . . . and why did she leave it for you—?"

It's a relief to finally hear someone else struggle.

"Hang on, you're saying you all had one?" Trinity asks, piecing it together. "And somehow Mya got Lucy's, and she left it for you," she says to me, and I nod.

"I know she was trying to tell me something," I say. "I just can't figure out what."

"Because she gave you a bracelet?" Trinity's giving me that look again, like she's worried for my mental health.

"Because she met me in the park one night," I say, and Maritza whips her head around, her cheeks red for some reason.

"Why?" she demands, and suddenly I feel defensive for no particular reason.

"I told you, because she was trying to tell me something," I say, and it comes out a little angrier than I mean for it to. It's just that no matter what I do, I can't seem to shake the guilt from that night, for letting her down.

"I just didn't listen," I say, a little calmer, and now we're all quiet.

"None of us did," Maritza says softly, and I have to swallow a giant lump in my throat to breathe again.

"So now what?" Trinity says what we're all thinking. Everything we have—everything I've gathered over the past three and a half months—amounts to nothing but take-out orders, weird sounds, and petty theft.

"We need more," I say, and Maritza and Trinity nod in silent agreement.

"It's not like this whole EarthPro thing is making things easier," Trinity says, and for a second, I'd actually forgotten about EarthPro. Now the thought of that fence around the factory and its nosy camera just feels like one more massive obstacle.

"It's all my parents talk about lately," I say, yet another thing I'm saying for the first time aloud. Maybe that's because this is the first time I've had people there to listen.

"Mine, too," Trinity says, rolling her eyes, which is

rare because if I ever thought my parents and I were tight, Trinity and her parents are like three adults sharing one giant brain. Mr. and Mrs. Bales work in human rights, and they take turns flying to countries that need things like clean drinking water. They're basically the kind of people Mrs. Tillman pretends to be. Which is why it's weird to see Trinity get impatient with the people she's normally so proud to talk about.

"They keep saying how this town needs to heal, which I guess is why they spend all their time at city council meetings now," she says.

"My dad's practically obsessed," Maritza says, and I'm surprised because I figured it was all pretty cut-and-dried for Mr. Esposito. A story is a story.

"It's almost like he feels responsible for the town," she says, and Trinity nods knowingly.

"He wants to be sure he's telling both sides of the story, but it's hard when you know no matter what you write, it's going to upset someone," she says, and I think back to my parents' argument from the other night, how my dad just wants to be a good journalist and my mom just wants to be a good scientist, and why shouldn't they both get to have what they want? Why does a company like EarthPro get to decide that?

"I keep going back to that aunt in Minnesota," Trinity says, shifting back to the Petersons. "I mean, why is everyone so willing to believe that? Why would they go away, but Mr. Peterson would stay?"

"Aaron never mentioned any aunt to me," I say.

Maritza chimes in. "Mya never said anything, either. If there really is an Aunt Lisa, I doubt she's anyone they'd want to go live with after their mom just died."

"Great," I say. "All we need to do is track down a mysterious Aunt Lisa. Shouldn't be too hard. How many Lisas do you suppose live in Minnesota?"

I walk over to my bed and slump down in defeat. It seems like the more we uncover about what's going on in the Peterson house, the less we know. I thought I understood Aaron. Then his mom died, and after the funeral, everything changed. Not that funerals are ever fun, but that one took horrible to a whole new level. Everything from Mr. Peterson freaking out in his room to Aaron basically telling me he never wanted to see me again to Mrs. Tillman and her fake smile calling me Nicholas like she knows me—

"Mrs. Tillman," I say, first to myself, then to Trinity and Maritza. "Mrs. Tillman!"

Trinity cocks her head.

"Crazy health food lady who owns the crunchy store," Maritza explains, and Trinity nods.

"She was hanging all over some woman at the funeral she called Lisa. I bet that was her!"

Maritza's eyes light up. "So, you just need to ask Mrs. Tillman if she knows how to get in touch with her!"

I shake my head. "Nope, not me."

"Oh, right."

We take a moment of silence for the audio synthesizer incident.

"We'll do it," Maritza says, and Trinity ponders for a minute, then nods.

"We'll go tomorrow, after school."

I nod, buoyed by a trace of hope. "I'll go back through my notebook to see if I've missed anything," I say.

"No, you won't," Maritza says.

"Huh?"

"You'll catch my brother up at the party Saturday night."

The *Raven Brooks Banner* holiday party. I completely forgot. My parents told me about it three weeks ago, and I promptly tucked it away deep into that part of my brain that hates getting dressed up for boring adult things.

"I can get out of it," I say, already feeling the creep of desperation at the back of my neck. "I'll just catch Enzo another time."

Trinity and Maritza shake their heads in unison.

"We need you to talk to Enzo about the paper. Convince him that the paper needs to hold off on writing any more EarthPro stories until we've had a chance to look around the park a little more."

"*Without* Mr. Peterson there," Maritza adds, stifling a shiver.

"Why me?" I ask. I'm whining, but I'm totally okay with it. "Why can't you talk to your dad?" I ask Maritza. Okay, I beg Maritza. Anything not to go to this party. I can already feel the pinch of my shoes.

"Because I've been telling him for weeks that EarthPro is going to drive all the small businesses out of Raven Brooks, and that hasn't made any difference," she says.

"Enzo would be a new voice in their dad's ear. If Enzo turns against EarthPro, too, his dad will start to feel out-numbered at home," Trinity agrees, and it appears she and Maritza have already given this part some thought.

"Besides," Maritza says, "you think I want to go to that party? I weaseled out of it weeks ago. You're the lucky duck who's already going."

If this is what luck feels like, I think I'd rather go back to being a loser.

Chapter 7

My nemesis. My archenemy. The water to my oil. The pin to my balloon.

I stare at my suit in the closet, and I swear to the Aliens it stares back at me, taunting me, lording its power over me because it knows what tonight is.

"Dad!" I holler, and he hustles into my room, toothbrush jutting from his mouth like a cigar. He's in boxers and a button-down shirt, his black socks pulled high.

"Well, you're alive," he says. He's been tense lately. This thing with Mr. Esposito is really eating at him.

"Sorry," I say. "It's just . . . do I have to wear it?"

"You know what your mom's going to say."

"I know, but this is *your* work party. Aren't you guys, like, more casual at the paper?"

"What'd'ya'rink—" He pulls the toothbrush from his mouth and tries again. "What do you think we do there all day, play foosball and eat donuts?"

We stare at each other for a minute because we both

know there's a good chance I could find a half-empty donut box in his office without trying too hard.

"I know how hard you and Mom work," I say more carefully this time. "I'm just saying that when you work, you wear T-shirts."

"Only when I have to go in at night," he says, still a little defensive. "And we're not working a late-breaking scoop," he says. "This is the holiday party."

"Dad," I say, one last desperate plea at my disposal. "It suffocates things." I lean in. "*Important* things."

Dad puts his hands up in surrender, his toothbrush a white flag. "A shirt and tie," he says. "Jeans and sneakers."

I open my mouth to protest, but he points his toothbrush at me, the white flag looking more like a gavel now.

"Shirt and tie. That's the compromise. And you're welcome."

He turns and walks away, looking pretty proud of himself even though his socks are high enough to crease his calves.

In the car, Mom looks better than both of us combined in her cranberry-colored skirt and white fluffy sweater. Dad must have thought I made a pretty compelling argument because he's wearing a shirt and tie with jeans and his favorite Converse. Normally, Mom would have rolled her eyes at us, but she knows how worked up my dad's been about tonight, so she just squeezes his hand and says, "You look great."

He smiles, and I try to push away the feeling that tonight is anything other than a stupid holiday party with boring grown-ups talking about boring grown-up things. But I can't erase the memory of the argument I overheard between my dad and Mr. Esposito—or rather, one half of the argument, even though it wasn't exactly hard to figure out what Enzo's dad was saying on the other end. The thing is, I don't think Mr. Esposito's wrong about Mr. Peterson being to blame for Lucy Yi's death. I just need him to hold off on being right a little bit longer.

When we pull up to the *Raven Brooks Banner* office, multicolored strings of blinking lights greet us from the lobby, and I tug at my tie a little too aggressively, pulling the knot down so it looks more like a necklace.

The lobby's marble floors are awash in red and yellow and green lights, the melody of "Winter Wonderland" bouncing off the walls like a racquetball. It's a sea of scruffy-faced men in wrinkled jeans and ties, women in skirts with static cling and hair pulled behind clips and combs in ways that look like they itch. Everyone is holding a cup with something yellow and fizzy, while they shift from one foot to the other, huddled and laughing, or huddled and gossiping, or huddled and staring into their fizzy cups. I scan the room for Enzo, and it doesn't take me long to find him, hovering around the plastic table with a smorgasbord of meatballs and pasta salad and gingersnaps.

"Took you long enough," he says, looking more relieved than annoyed, which in turn relieves me since we didn't part ways on the best of terms earlier this week. I still can't get used to his hair, though. The gel looks thick enough to feel heavy. I wonder if he's struggling to keep his head up.

"What's that?" I say, pointing to the only thing I can't identify on the table. It's not quite brown, not quite yellow, maybe a custard of some kind, but with an unsettling smattering of blackish dots.

"I don't know," Enzo says, looking concerned. "But I bumped the table a minute ago, and it jiggled."

We each suppress a shiver and scoop a handful of gingersnaps and three triangles apiece of baklava.

"Hey, what kind of triangle is this?" Enzo snorts as we head for a corner of the room.

It's from there that I hear Mr. Esposito call out for my dad.

"Ah, you've decided to honor us with your presence, huh?" he says like he's joking, but he's the only one who laughs.

Dad gives him a handshake-hug like always, but they both break away quickly.

"Luanne, you look exquisite as always," Miguel says, pulling my mom in for a hug, and she smiles.

"I was promised baklava and all the Christmas carols I can stand." She may not have grown up celebrating Christmas, but my mom is a certified holiday music aficionado. The day after Thanksgiving, when the local soft rock station starts playing Christmas songs 24-7, is like its own holiday in our house, when Mom bops around the house singing songs most people are sick to death of by the time they're adults.

Even if she weren't excited about the music or the desserts, though, Mom would find some other way to make Dad feel less anxious about arguing with his boss and wrestling with his conscience.

Standing next to Enzo as we stuff our faces with gingersnaps, I wish Mom had some magic trick for making me feel less like I was going to puke. I'm counting out in my head all the things I need to say that could tick off Enzo: the fact that I won't let go of Aaron and Mya's disappearance, the fact that I want his help convincing his dad to lay off the Mr. Peterson stories until we've had a chance to gather more evidence, the fact that I've been hanging out with his sister and his girlfriend while we spy on the possibly bonkers neighbor who lives across the street from me . . .

And because I'm terrible at making decisions, or terrible at timing, or light-headed from my tie, or tired from too many nights spent wandering in my sleep—I tell him everything. All at once.

"Here's the thing. I've been watching Mr. Peterson a lot. A lot. And he knows something about Aaron and Mya that he's not telling anyone. I'm positive of it, and Maritza knows it, too, so she and Trinity are going to talk to Mrs. Tillman to check up about the whole aunt-in-Minnesota story, but we think he's hiding something over at the old amusement park, and we want to look for clues, but we can't if EarthPro goes and digs everything up, so we need your help convincing your dad to stop running the stories Mrs. Yi wants him to run so we can find what we need to help Aaron and Mya."

I take a massive breath and shove an entire triangle of baklava into my mouth. It's the first time I've said everything to Enzo, and I can't believe how amazing it feels to unload the burden that's been slowly suffocating me for months. I feel something I haven't felt since Aaron disappeared, something I thought I'd forgotten how to feel—I feel good about myself. Finally, I'm doing something that maybe, just maybe, can help Aaron and Mya.

When I turn to face Enzo, though, the weight on my chest returns, heavier than it was before, and it brought a friend: fear. Because Enzo looks like he's ready to punch me in the face.

"It wasn't just a coincidence in the woods, was it? You've been bringing my little sister around that creep I told her never to go near again."

Oh no. Oh Aliens. It's possible I should have put some more thought around how I said all that out loud.

"And now you're telling me you sent my little sister and my girlfriend to talk to that wingnut at the natural grocer who has the police on speed dial and hates kids, to collect evidence for your conspiracy theory?"

Enzo is stronger than me. Way stronger. But I've beat him in wind sprints. I think given the proper motivation, I could outrun him.

"And after all that, you want me to convince my dad that, even though a little girl died, it's okay and no one should have to pay for it. We should just go on pretending like we're all over what happened. He should keep publishing stories about how Mrs. Poulson trained her cat how to high-five, and no one should worry that we're the only city in the entire state that doesn't have a Buy Mart."

"Wait, what?" I say. He lost me at the high-fiving cat.

"EarthPro, genius," he says. I'm keeping a close eye on the hand he's starting to ball into a fist at his side. "They want to build a Buy Mart. Anyway, you're not getting it. There's more at stake here than your stupid suspicions about your freaky neighbor. You're new, so I'm going to give you a pass, but you don't know what it's like to grow up here. Some of us actually hate driving an hour to get normal groceries. Some of us want to play sports and be able to hang out somewhere—*anywhere*—that doesn't remind you of the girl who died. Some of us just want to be normal."

I can't even taste the baklava anymore. I think I swallowed it, but I can't tell because there's this huge lump in my throat that's making it hard to breathe.

If I came here thinking Enzo was my friend, that he was ever my friend, then I've just been fooling myself. I'm not the normal kid he wants to be, and I'm definitely not the normal kid he wants hanging around him.

"Just back off of it, okay?" he says, but he's not really asking. "Back off of this whole Mr. Peterson thing. Back off of this whole Aaron-and-Mya mystery that you've invented."

Then he turns to fully face me.

"And back off of my sister. Trinity just feels sorry for you, but Lucy was Maritza's friend. You don't have a clue about what she's gone through, and all you're doing is making her relive it."

I heard somewhere that the human body is made up of over 60 percent water, but I never really believed it until this moment, when I feel like I've been hit by a massive wave and I'm drowning under it. And no matter how much I flail, I can't find the surface, I can't find air. I can't even tell if I'm trying anymore.

Enzo didn't have to take a swing at my face. All he had to do was open his mouth.

"Ladies and gentlemen, if I can have your attention, please!" Mr. Esposito bellows into the crowd, but I can barely hear him over the rushing tide.

"I'd like to introduce a very special guest tonight. Many of you already know her through her work with the city council, and most recently, her work with the state's attorney's office. As you know, we here at the *Raven Brooks Banner* are closely following the EarthPro story with a special focus on how their arrival in our beautiful town impacts our community. And while many of us fall on opposing sides of the question of development, I think we can all agree that our friend Brenda Yi has been invaluable in advocating tirelessly for the best interests of Raven Brooks. And speaking of developments, Brenda's just told me she has some news she'd like to share. And you know

I'm never one to pass up an exclusive," Mr. Esposito says to the room that's suddenly grown lively.

"Take a night off, Miguel!" someone bellows, and Mr. Esposito chuckles.

"You take enough nights off for us all, Barry," he retorts, and the room erupts with laughter.

"Thank you, Miguel," Mrs. Yi says, nodding to her friend, and the room hushes because Mrs. Yi demands a certain respect. It occurs to me that I've never even seen her before, but somehow, she's not at all what I expected. Her hair is smoothed back into a bun, little streaks of gray weaving through the sleek black strands. She's small in size, but not in presence; her quiet voice carries with deep resonance, and while her face is pretty, the skin around her eyes hangs loosely, like she's tired from fighting a never-ending battle.

"I'll keep this quick, and before I say anything, I just want to thank you all for the work you've been doing here at the paper to cover this story fairly and thoroughly. I recognize that the EarthPro issue has become a divisive one, but in this time of holiday celebration, I hope we can all set aside our differences and remember that part of what makes Raven Brooks such a special town is its allowance for differing opinions."

The room stays silent, which is why I can hear Enzo sniff next to me, and it's the meanest sniff I've ever heard. He's sniffing at me.

"I'd like to share with you that the council has decided to grant EarthPro permission to excavate the land previously owned by the Golden Apple Corporation."

She pauses for a moment before adding, "*All* the land."

A few people cough, some whisper, but mostly, the room remains motionless and quiet, and everyone lets Mrs. Yi speak because she's more than paid for this silence.

"For those who are reticent to allow EarthPro into our fine city, I want you to know that you'll have ample opportunity to make your concerns known. The city council will bar development for ninety days while we field questions at a series of town halls; however, barring any substantial argument to the contrary, the town will move forward with clearing the land and redeveloping in three months."

As Mrs. Yi finishes her remarks, there are a few things I see while I'm flailing under the weight of Enzo's threat and this new wave of information. I see Dad move a little closer to Mom, her hand already extended to hold his before he even reaches out. I see a man with a scruffy beard toward the back of the room nodding in agreement with the things Mrs. Yi isn't saying because she's trying to sound impartial. I see a woman next to him look at the ground instead of disagreeing with him while he silently agrees. I see a weird empty space suddenly created in the room, an aisle that forms almost by accident, but on one side there are more people nodding like the scruffy-bearded man, and there are people on the other side of the expanse looking hard at the people who are nodding, or looking down, or looking at the drinks in their hands that have stopped fizzing.

But mostly I see Mr. Esposito looking at Mrs. Yi and caring. Really caring. I'm not sure if he cares about her or what she's been through or EarthPro or the *Raven Brooks Banner.* But he cares just as deeply as my dad cares about integrity, and so does everyone in the room.

Except for maybe Enzo because I'm drowning right here next to him and it doesn't seem to bother him a bit.

The minute the music comes back on, the expanse in the middle of the room fills with people again, and someone's singing about Mommy kissing Santa Claus, and someone else is pointing and laughing at two people standing under the mistletoe hanging in the doorway to the break room, and someone else just knocked into the table and made the gelatin thing jiggle, and that's when I finally turn to Enzo.

Because I've found the surface of the stupid ocean and breathing has never felt better.

"You know what you are?" I ask him, but I don't wait for an answer. "You're a coward."

Enzo turns to face me now, and his hands start balling into fists again, but I couldn't care less because I'm faster, and being fast is way better than being strong.

"Say that again?" he says, and I think maybe he actually didn't hear me.

"You're a coward. It's easier for you to talk about wanting to be normal, whatever that means, than to do something to help your friend."

"You don't know what you're talking about," Enzo says, and his hands loosen by his sides, but his ears and neck are getting all splotchy.

"You saw firsthand what Aaron and Mya were going through, and what did you do?"

Enzo squares his jaw.

"Nothing," I say, because now that I've started, I can't stop. "You turned your back on them and played your video games in your big fancy house like nothing had ever happened. Now I'm asking you for your help, and you're doing the same thing. Turning your back on me. And for what? So you can be friends with Seth and Ruben?"

"What's wrong with Seth and Ruben?" he asks, and he can barely get his question out before I bark a laugh that sounds mean even to me.

"Seriously? Seth Gruber? Dude, he choked on his own loogie."

"It wasn't that serious. They were just having a spitting contest."

"He had to go to the hospital," I say.

"So, he has thick snot. It's not a crime."

"Ruben thinks that sheep are just goats with more hair."

"Not everyone has to be a genius. What, you think you're so brilliant? You believe in aliens!"

"There's a difference between plausible hypothesis and provable fact. Come on, man! Sheep and goats?"

"You're just jealous."

"Oh yeah, I'm jealous. I wish I could dribble a ball and choke on my own spit."

"Maybe you just can't stand to see me make friends because you think I'm a loser loner like you. Maybe you wouldn't know the first thing about making friends because you've never stuck around long enough to prove you're not a *total freak*."

The water's back, washing over me in huge, suffocating waves. I keep opening my mouth to disagree, but all I taste is salt. I wish I was the type of person whose hands curled into fists like Enzo's do, but all my hands do is fall at my sides, useless and lifeless while I let the water knock me around.

"Narf!" I hear Dad call to me from someplace far away, or maybe he's right next to me. I can't tell anymore.

"Hey, Narf, say bye to Enzo—it's time to head home," Dad says, and now I know he's beside me because I can hear the concern in his voice, but I don't look at my dad. I don't move at all, not until he takes my mom's hand and starts to walk toward the door that faces the parking lot.

I turn to go and I almost don't say anything else, but after I've taken a couple steps away from Enzo, I can breathe again, and this time the air doesn't taste good. This time, it just tastes . . . empty.

"Have fun with your new friends," I say.

As soon as I have my back to him, I hear him say, "Have fun alone."

Then I'm outside. Then I'm in the car. Then I'm home, in bed, with nothing but silence and the giant empty hole where friends should be.

But I'm not the type of kid to have friends, not really. Not if I'm being honest. If I'm being honest, Enzo's right. I'm the same kid I was when I moved here from Charleston, and when I moved there from Ontario, Oakland, Redding. I'm Nate, or Nat, or Ned, the kid whose hair sticks up in funny places and wears shirts with jokes nobody gets, and really, I was fooling myself if I thought that friendship was ever going to be my thing.

Except, for one summer, it *was* my thing. But I couldn't even make that last.

Really, I was fooling myself if I thought I was anything more than a shell that gets nudged around by the waves, hoping one day I'll land far enough from the water to get buried by the sand.

Chapter 8

There are so many ways to avoid people.

There are socks to be paired and binocuscopes to fix and homework to do. I never help Mom with the grocery shopping, and something should be done about that. And Dad's office isn't going to vacuum itself.

"Narf, it's not that I don't appreciate the inexplicable wave of good deeds we're experiencing here," Dad says one day in late January as he lifts his feet over the vacuum I run underneath his chair.

"Huh? Can't hear you, Dad!" I call over the roar. This is the very conversation I've managed to dodge for the better part of winter break, and I don't intend to have that chat now.

Instead of yelling over the vacuum, though, Dad gets clever and waits me out. He knows that I'm going to have to finish the room at some point; there's only so much carpet. Then I'll have to turn off the vacuum and face the sentence my dad is going to repeat. If he's decided to bring it up, he's going to see it through. Dad treats a tough topic like a boomerang. He only throws it out there if he's ready for it to swing back.

I finish the job because I hate leaving a project undone. Then I switch off the vacuum and begin wrapping the cord, waiting for the inevitable.

"How bad is it?" he asks.

I look at him. "Bad."

"On a scale of 'I stubbed my toe' to 'I accidentally blew up the universe'?" He waits for me.

"Hold on, what makes you think it's something *I* did?" I ask.

"Because you're the one who hasn't left the house for three and a half weeks, and at least two different nice-sounding people have called you."

I'd ask, but I already know it's Maritza and Trinity. If Enzo had called, Dad would have told me. Which means he knows the issue is partly Enzo.

"So, why'd you tell Mom to tell Mr. Esposito you weren't here when he called last night?" I ask, and now I bet Dad's wishing he had his own vacuuming to do.

"Okay, look," he says, leaning forward on his desk while he rubs a wrinkle from his forehead. "I'm going to level with you. Mr. Esposito and I . . . we're not on the best terms right now." And even though that's not exactly the shock of the century, Dad seems a little stunned to hear himself say it. "But here's the thing. I know exactly why it is we're butting heads. And even though we're stuck in this place now, I believe that we'll get past it."

I stare at him, and when he doesn't tell me, I ask, "How do you know you'll get past it?"

Dad's quiet for a minute. "Because if you're friends, you agree on at least one thing: You want to be friends."

He doesn't know it, but Dad's just shattered me because Enzo doesn't want to be my friend anymore. He told me so.

"What if one of you is bad at being a friend?" I ask, because apparently I'm in the mood to torture myself.

Dad smiles, which is a weird way to react to the end of the world.

"We're all bad at being friends," he says, taking the vacuum and rolling it to the hall closet. "The best part of being a friend is trying to be a better one."

* * *

These days, I spend most of my nights trying to fall asleep, and then regretting when I do.

This dream isn't like the others. I can tell right away I'm inside, but not in a shopping cart or roller coaster car. This time, I'm on cold, hard cement.

"Hello?"

My voice should come back to me. Surrounded by all

this cement, I expect an echo, but I'm greeted only by thick silence, like the air has swallowed my word in one gulp.

Then, all at once, a voice does waft past my ear: not my echo, but the familiar croaking voice of my long-dead grandmother.

"You stop that wandering, Boychik! Or one day, you won't make it home!"

It's the only thing I ever remember her saying. There were kind words and strong hugs I'm sure, but her warning is all that's stayed with me. It didn't work, though. My dreams make me wander; they always have.

Slowly, light creeps in, and I see I'm in the Golden Apple factory, its endless hallway of locked doors lined up on either side of me, bearing witness to Aaron's and my petty crimes. I don't have my lockpicks with me, though, so I pound on door after door down the endless corridor. No one answers.

Finally reaching the end of the hallway, I come to a door that's different than the others. This one is wooden, with boards nailed across the front and a series of locks dangling from their hinges. I pull the boards away and pry off what remains of the hinged locks, then open the door to a set of steep stairs descending into an inky depth I can't see the bottom of.

"Aaron!" I call, but barely a sound comes out. I try again.

"Mya!" But my voice is lost to the same echoless abyss as before.

I know I shouldn't go through the door, but my grandma was right; I wander where I'm not supposed to, and this time, I think where I'm not supposed to go is exactly where I'll find the answers to where Aaron and Mya are.

Bracing myself against the cold cement walls, I grope for a railing that doesn't exist and instead tap my toe in front of me to find each steep step that leads me farther into the bowels of what feels less like the Golden Apple factory and more like whatever lies behind the forbidden cellar door of the Petersons' house.

The steps in my dream are getting steeper, and soon I can't feel the next one with my toe. I hold my breath as I drop down with each descent, and the walls have gone from cool and dry to slick with some sort of dark grease.

Then, on the last step, the ground doesn't meet me like it should. I try to pull myself back against the wall, but it's too slick, and I fall with a stumble, skidding face-first to the damp, cold floor.

I'm surrounded in a darkness so thick, I can't see my hand in front of me.

"Aaron?" I call, but again, the sound of my voice barely carries from my lips, absorbed in the same darkness that covers me.

"Anyone?"

And here's when it first occurs to me: If I'm in a dream, why can't I wake up? And if this isn't a dream . . . no one knows I'm here.

No one is looking for me.

"Hello!" I call. "Anyone? HELLO!" I yell, but there's no one there to hear my pleas.

The air at the bottom of this place is different—stale and old, like it's been breathed a thousand times already. I crawl on the cold floor until the sound of my labored breathing fades under a different sound—the faint notes of a motorized organ, the kind piped through the machinery of a carousel.

A brown flicker of candlelight emerges from the distance, growing to orange and then to yellow, and in the light I find myself again in the wire shopping cart. I know where this dream is going now, and I want desperately to close my eyes, to find myself in the light, under the sun and the clouds and the breeze of fresh, clean air. Instead, I'm lifted in my shopping cart like I always am, the gears of machinery working hard in the darkness, and I rise so high so fast, I feel my stomach drop. Below me, I see the dim flicker of more and more candles, and the movement of tiny ant people.

"Someone! Please someone help!" I shout to them.

But when they look up at me, their heads tilting to the sky in unison, every single face is blank, like their features have been wiped away.

I keep rising and rising until the machinery jolts to a sudden stop. Then, with no warning, the cart tips forward and empties me into the faceless crowd below.

I scream all the way down as pale hands reach to welcome me into their expressionless masses. I fight and flail my way through the bodies and clamber for the cold floor I'd been so desperate to escape before.

Then, through a tinny speaker somewhere high above, I hear a voice warped by the broken speaker say: "Do you like it? I built it. It's all for you, children."

And then the voice breaks, and its low tones give way to a high, breathy laugh that makes the floor under me feel warm in comparison.

"Let me out!" I scream. "I want to go home!"

The room goes quiet, and the candles are suddenly snuffed out. It's so still and so dark, for a moment I think I've fought my way free of whatever evil has managed to grip me.

Then, from the inky darkness, the voice is suddenly inches from my ear: "You are home."

I gasp awake, and spittle catches in my throat, making me cough and sputter. I reach for the glass of water I've kept by my bed for as long as I can remember, but somewhere in the midst of my flailing, I knock it over, sending it flying hard enough to hit the edge of my dresser and shatter.

I hear Dad curse, then a thud. Mom's raspy voice talks over his, muffled. Dad grumbles, and I hear the soft padding of Mom's feet as she makes her way down the hall into my room. I'm trying to scoop up the shards by moonlight.

"Oh, Narf, what's this?"

"I knocked it over," I say, and she crouches beside me to pick up the smaller pieces my shaking fingers can't grasp. Then she takes the bigger shards from me and nudges my hands away gently, protecting me from cuts. After she wipes up the water with a sponge from the bathroom, she eases onto the edge of my bed and pulls the covers to my chin, a gesture that means more than she could possibly understand because she hasn't done that since I was five.

"You had a nightmare," she tells me rather than asks. She sounds stern, and I think she's probably mad about the glass, or maybe about me waking Dad and her up.

"I don't know," I say, doing my best to shrug it off, but I'm still shaking even after all that time spent cleaning up.

"You've been having those a lot," she says, again stern, but this time she puts her hand over my forehead like she's checking me for a fever. I catch her glancing at the window that faces the Petersons' house.

"It's not a big deal," I tell her, and it's a waste of a lie.

She stares at me for a long time, and I stare back at her because it seems like the right thing to do.

"What's it about?" she asks me, and I start to feel hot all of a sudden. She pulls her hand away from my forehead like she feels the heat, and this time, I know exactly why I'm staring at her and she's staring at me: She doesn't need to ask me what my dream was about. She already knows.

"The grocery store?"

I stop breathing.

"In through your nose, out through your mouth, Narf," she says, and I do it because she's my mom, and she knows better.

When I don't feel like I'm going to pass out anymore, I say, "How do you know that?"

She looks like she's about to stand up. Her muscles get tense, and she's got her hands on the edge of the bed like she's bracing herself to flee. But she looks at the floor instead, and I wonder if she's found a shard of glass that we missed.

After a long time, she says, "Your Bubbe had . . . worries."

It occurs to me that Mom has never talked about my grandmother outside of logistics. First there was making sure to call her every Saturday night so Grandma (who Mom called Bubbe) wouldn't be offended. Then it was getting her moved into our house after she got too old to live alone. Then it was making sure Grandma took all her medication. After she died, there were more things to do: making funeral arrangements, cleaning out her room, deciding who would get the antique lace she came over with from Poland.

There was the business of mourning her death, which Mom did dutifully.

But after all the work was done, we never really talked about Grandma. We don't keep a single picture of her anywhere in the house. I think about the beautiful pictures of Mrs. Esposito that Enzo and his family keep on their mantel in celebration of her memory, and I search my mind for Grandma's memorial. It doesn't exist. All I know about my grandmother are the memories I've kept zipped up in my pocket, closely guarded because whatever she said to me felt like a secret that had to be protected. I never understood why, but I never asked, either. Grandma knew things. She knew things I knew, and she knew things I was afraid to know.

And now, for the first time in my life, I'm seeing that Mom must have known these things, too.

"What happened?" I ask my mom, and she just stares at the floor. I get braver. "What happened *to me*?"

Mom looks at me, her eyes welling, which is something because Mom never cries. "She understood you," Mom says. "Better than anyone, I think."

I keep watching her, waiting for the "but." Grandma was a lot of things, but "understanding" was not a word I'd associate with the woman who instilled more fear in me than my most terrifying nightmare.

"She understood you, which is why she worried about you," Mom says, and her forehead crinkles as she loses herself in a memory I can't see. "She used to call you a *wolf.*"

I remember that much. I thought it was cool at first: She thought I was a sly hunter with a keen instinct. Soon, though, I realized she meant that I was wild, that I was destined to be alone. I would never fit into a pack if I kept wandering.

"See, Bubbe was led by the old ways," Mom says, trying to soften the perception of me in Grandma's eyes. "She thought imaginative kids were . . . um . . ." Mom struggles before she lands on the kindest word: "vulnerable."

"She thought I was weak," I say, too tired to sugarcoat.

"Not weak," Mom insists. "She thought you were in danger."

I roll my eyes because that's not any different than weak.

"She thought you were a danger to yourself," she says, and then she pauses while I contemplate the difference between a wuss and being too adventurous for my own good.

"But I didn't do anything," I say, and then clarify, "back then."

Mom tries to hide her smile. She doesn't want to encourage me. We don't talk about Mrs. Tillman or what happened there, not after Mrs. Peterson's accident.

Instead she says, "You had this tendency to . . . wander."

"In my sleep," I say.

Mom cocks her head. "Not in your sleep. You drifted. You would get lost in your own thoughts, and you would . . . I don't know, wander off."

"So? All kids do that," I say defensively.

She stifles another smile. "Not like you did. You had a special knack."

Then her smile fades, and I consider for a second that she knows how my dreams have led me back to my wandering ways at night. But there's no chance. She would have barricaded me in my room if she knew that.

No, there's another reason my mom has stopped smiling.

"She did something," Mom says. Then, out of nowhere, she starts to cry. Not just the teary eyes that she had a second ago, but actual weeping. She covers her face like she can hide it, but it's way too late for that. I want to make her feel better, but I feel frozen. I've never seen her do this before, and whatever she'd said up to this point that made me feel better slips away because seeing your parents cry inverts your world for a minute.

"Your dad and I, we went away for a weekend. We *needed* a weekend." She says the second part defensively, and I try to figure out what I did to put her defenses up.

"She told me and told me. She told me so many times," Mom says, shaking her head slowly. "She said, 'He wanders. He will get himself hurt if he keeps wandering like that.'"

Mom wipes her face hard enough to leave pink smears on her cheeks. "You have to understand, Nicky: By then, your bubbe had started to . . . uh . . . lose it a little."

Grandma hadn't just lost it by the time I was old enough to register her scolding voice and accusatory finger. She was completely off her nut.

"When your dad and I got home," Mom says slowly, head down and mumbling by this point, "Bubbe was here, just . . . sitting on the edge of the couch like she was waiting."

Mom looks confused, like to this day, the memory baffles her. Then her face crumples, and oh Aliens, I think she's going to cry again. She fights it off, though, and speeds her way through the rest.

"You weren't in the house. We asked her and asked her where you were. Finally, I grabbed her by the shoulders and God help me I smacked her face like she was a child and—"

"Did Grandma leave me at the grocery store?"

Mom turns to me, holding my face between her hands so my lips puff out. "You were three years old. My God, I never forgave her for that. She left you there in the back room."

She releases my face and covers her mouth, then collects herself, and this time I know it's for good. After this, Mom won't talk about it again.

"I think in her own way, she really thought she was keeping you safe . . . teaching you that if you wander, sometimes you can't find your way back. Sometimes, you get—"

"Lost," I say.

Mom gives me that look again like she's trying to see through me. I smile at her so she'll stop trying.

"It's fine, Mom," I say, even though it's not.

She puts her hand over my forehead again, and now I think I understand that she's trying to read my thoughts. Or maybe clear my thoughts away so she can replace them with happy ones. I wish it were that simple.

"I don't wander so much anymore," I say, and this lie isn't wasted. I know it will make Mom feel better, even if she doesn't fully believe me. But I'm tired, and I know she is, too.

"Go to sleep, Narf," she says, and kisses me hard on the head where her hand was seconds ago.

I want her to go back to her bed, but she curls up at the foot of mine instead. She says it's because she's waiting until I fall asleep again, but I think she can't leave yet, not with that confession still looming in the air. Most people feel better after they let go of a secret that massive, but it seems like Mom actually feels worse. I think maybe it's because you can't keep a secret that toxic without it burning a hole in you after a while. And guilt is horrible at filling holes.

I don't blame Mom, though. Strangely, I don't blame Grandma, either. If Mom was right—if my grandmother really understood me in a way no one else could—then all she was trying to do was protect me. I look at my hands for the first time in the dawning daylight and see what I couldn't possibly have seen earlier as I carefully placed shards of glass in my palms—I see dark smears of grease. Just like the grease from the walls that I tried to brace myself against in my dream before I fell down the steep steps into . . . wherever it was I fell into. I wandered again before I woke from my nightmare, only this time, I have no idea where I went.

Grandma's grocery store idea might not have worked, but at least she tried. If she was trying to save me from this new living nightmare, then in some ways, I love her more now than I was ever able to love her when she was alive and scaring the pee out of me.

When I finally fall asleep again, Mom is still curled at the foot of my bed. Which is why when I hear rustling before I open my eyes to the fully broken daylight, I figure it's just her. But my feet move freely, and squinting one eye open, I see only crumpled sheets at the foot of my bed.

"Aaron," I breathe before I realize what I'm saying.

I'm on my feet with lightning speed and snapping the screen from my bedroom window just as the rustling stops. Sure enough, a fluttering piece of notebook paper flaps at the bottom of the vines that climb the front of our turquoise house.

The trellis creaks under my weight, but I don't care. If it breaks, I'll help my dad fix it later. All I can focus on is the thrumming of my heart and the fact that Aaron was just here. Who else would have left me a note in our spot?

When I reach the ground, I unfold the paper, and my heart stops its pounding and drops to my feet. I slump to the front lawn, and I don't care that it's freezing and the rain from last night is soaking through my flannel pajama pants. I don't care about much of anything because I can tell right away that this isn't Aaron's handwriting.

It's tidier and slants neatly to the right, a perfect cursive script.

Sorry, but you wouldn't answer any of our calls, Dummy. We need to talk. IT'S IMPORTANT. Meet us at the Farmers' Market tomorrow. Seriously.

Chapter 9

I guess I deserve the harsh note Maritza and Trinity left me, but when I slouch through the crowd the next day, I can't keep myself from glaring at the two of them for tricking me into responding.

"Who has farmers' markets during the winter anyway?" I grumble, and Maritza slides a paper bowl of chocolate-covered bananas in front of me as an apology.

"Look, if you haven't figured out by now that Raven Brooks is bizarro world, then there's no hope left for you," Trinity says, handing me a fork.

I eat the bananas because they're delicious and slowly forget my grudge, remembering how nice it is to know that even after the blowout fight with Enzo, I still have two friends left in the world. I start to fill them in about what happened at the party a few weeks ago, but they already know.

"Enzo will get over it," Maritza says, expertly avoiding taking sides, and I don't believe her, but I appreciate her saying it.

"He got *Punch Club* for Christmas," Trinity says. "I keep beating him, so he's tired of playing it with me."

"Did you guys have any luck with Mrs. Tillman?" I ask midbite.

Trinity and Maritza exchange glances. "'Luck' isn't necessarily the word I'd use."

"I mean," Maritza cuts in, "we may not have done anything to her, but we're *friends* with the people who destroyed her property and caused her to have a breakdown."

"Breakdown?" Trinity says, lifting an eyebrow at Maritza.

"Well, she had to go back to that silent meditation retreat in Santa Fe so she could calm down," Maritza says.

"Okay, first of all, she didn't *have* to go there. She used the money on a vacation instead of on a new sound system, and second, do we need to send you off to meditation camp, too? *Calm down.*"

Maritza rolls her eyes. "We asked Mrs. Tillman about the mysterious Aunt Lisa, and after a lot of yelling at us for what *you* did . . . she said she was just being nice to Lisa at the funeral. 'Following the voice of her heart' or some other touchy-feely mumbo jumbo."

"So, that's it," I say, suddenly losing interest in my banana.

She lifts her eyebrow at me, but by my count, we're no closer to figuring out a way to track down the mysterious

Aunt Lisa and stop EarthPro from decimating the park than we were a month ago.

Except Maritza's a step ahead of me. "I know you think we struck out," she says, and I'm dying for her to prove me wrong. "But Trinity got Mrs. Tillman talking about who else might have the number, and she mentioned that the only person she knew who'd have it was Mrs. Peterson herself . . ."

Trinity and Maritza exchange a glance, then lean in.

"What do you know about a flower-covered address book?"

I search my memory for anything flowery or address-bookish.

Then my mind rests on the Petersons' kitchen, the window where Mrs. Peterson used to sip her iced tea, whistling a sad song out the window or calling to Mya through the window over the sink. Occasionally, she would be on the phone, her voice rich and full and so different than the careful, measured tone she would use around Mr. Peterson.

And occasionally, as she was shifting the phone into the crook of her shoulder, her iced tea would spill onto the open address book beside the base of the phone, the book with the lettered tabs that held the phone numbers of those people she would call.

I stand, nearly knocking over my paper bowl.

"Her address book!" I say. Then I sit back down, eat the rest of my chocolate-dipped bananas in two bites, and look at Maritza and Trinity. "First, you're brilliant," I say, and they nod because they are.

"Second, we need to find a way to get into that house."

The girls exchange another conspiratorial look, and it's suddenly clear that while I've been looking for ways to avoid civilization this past month, they've been scheming to find ways into the Peterson house—ways that don't include sleep "wandering."

"We're going to need your picks, your binder, and your binocuscope," says Maritza.

"Buckle up, buttercup," says Trinity. "This ride could get bumpy."

Chapter 10

It's one week later that I realize I'm dumb. I'm dumber than dumb. I must be to even consider doing what I'm about to do. And this time, I have accomplices, which means either I've turned Maritza and Trinity dumb, or they're even smarter evil geniuses than Aaron, and frankly that's terrifying.

"Tell me again that this is the only way," I say.

"This is the only way," Trinity says.

"Tell me in a way that makes me believe it," I say.

"You're stalling," Maritza says, and that confirms it. She's smarter.

"Look, I'd love to spend all day convincing you that this is a good idea, but according to your log, we've got less than an hour before Mr. Peterson comes home," Trinity says.

The plan is simple enough. It's a three-person operation, with two people acting as the lookout from separate vantage points and one finding a way inside, though we've opted to call it a "rescue operation" to sidestep the obvious fact that what we're doing is undeniably wrong.

Anyway, while Trinity is on the binocuscope, keeping an eye on the long view from my bedroom, Maritza is on the ground, taking cues from Trinity if trouble comes. That leaves me to focus on getting in through the front door, making my way to the kitchen, finding and copying down Aunt Lisa's number from the address book by the phone, and slipping back out, all before Mr. Peterson returns from his three o'clock Sunday drive. Even though I don't know exactly where it is he goes, I've told myself it's to see his wife's grave. Maybe it forces me see him as something more than a monster in an argyle sweater. All I know for sure is that he leaves every Sunday, and today is Sunday, so this is our chance.

I check my watch: 3:14 p.m.

"We have forty-five minutes," I say, and Maritza sighs impatiently.

"So, can we move this along?"

Just then, the phone in the kitchen rings, making us all jump.

"We don't have time for this," Maritza pleads.

"If it's my parents, they're going to keep calling until I answer," I say. "They have that town hall tonight. They're probably just making sure I know how to heat up the casserole for dinner."

It isn't my parents about the casserole, though. It's Trinity's parents about civic duty.

"Civic what?" I ask after I take the phone back from a dejected Trinity.

"Civic duty. They're making me go to the town hall with them."

"Now? But . . . why?" Maritza pleads, pacing across my kitchen floor.

"They believe in participation," she says, like that explains it, but this much is clear: The plan is off without Trinity.

"We'll do it next weekend," she says, and she's just as disappointed as we are, so I don't say that next weekend might be too late for Aaron and Mya.

On her way out the door, Trinity turns to look us both in the eye, a thought suddenly occurring to her.

"Wait for me," she says, almost scolding. "It's too dangerous without three of us."

Maritza and I nod, but neither of us says anything.

As soon as I close the door, Maritza stares me down, her round brown eyes boring through my skull.

"No," I say. "No, no, no. She's right. You know she's right. It's way too dangerous, Maritza."

"And you know this can't wait," she says, her gaze intensifying.

"We need a lookout," I argue, but I'm already starting to cave.

"I'll be the lookout!"

"I need you on the ground!"

Maritza takes a step toward me even though she's already pretty close, and now I'm sweating again. Why am I sweating? Can she see me sweating? Can she *smell* me?

"Nicky, you're the one who made me a believer. You're the reason I understand why they need us now."

I know it's a tactic. She's making me feel guilty. If anyone understands guilt, it's me. That doesn't mean it isn't working, though.

"And you know as well as I do that every day that goes by is another day they might be in trouble. Every day is another day that whatever evidence creepy Mr. Peterson might be hiding out there in that park might get dug up and destroyed forever because now, all of a sudden, the town wants to build a Buy Mart and forget the Petersons ever had kids in the first place!"

How is she so good at laying on the guilt?

"We have a plan, and it's a good one. We start with Aunt Lisa. We find out if Aaron and Mya are really with her. If they are, then we've done all this for nothing, and we can all be glad that we did this for nothing. If they're not . . ."

I sigh. "If they're not, then we know he's hiding something."

I don't say what it is Mr. Peterson could be hiding. I can't make myself say that part yet.

Maritza nods. "We're going in."

We spend a couple minutes on the porch rehearsing the plan. For the most part, it's still the same. We stay low to make sure no one is coming. Then Maritza crosses the street casually, slinking behind the remains of Mr. Peterson's white picket fence. A minute later, I trace the same path, only I duck behind two desks randomly stacked beside the driveway. Maritza moves in from there, dragging the garbage can from the fence to the door so it shields me from passersby who might see me picking the lock. Then Maritza takes cover by the fence again.

Originally, this is where Maritza would have taken her cues from Trinity as our eyes from the air, so to speak. Now, with only Maritza's vantage point from the ground, we're either going to have to be a lot more careful or go a lot faster.

Or both.

Maritza checks her watch. "Three twenty-five. We need to move."

And before I can make one more half-hearted argument to wait for Trinity, Maritza crosses the street, stealth as a ninja and fast enough to make me lose track of her for a second. All of a sudden, something between a yowl and a scream cuts through the air. A gray cat skitters to the sidewalk, back bent and ears low, hissing toward the fence before darting across the street and disappearing into a neighboring bush.

Maritza's head pops out from behind the fence. She shakes out her hair and peers down both ends of the street before waving me over. It feels like a high stakes game of Red Rover, and a nervous giggle trickles out of my mouth as I reach the tree beneath Aaron's window.

"You sound insane," she whispers.

"You *look* insane," I hiss back.

She shushes me and lifts a second garbage can, obscuring me behind the barrel before scurrying back to the fence.

Halfway across the yard, she turns back to me. "Remember, if you hear a tap on the glass——"

"Right. Get out."

Then she takes cover behind the fence until I can pick the lock. I fumble in my back pocket and grab my kit in its soft leather pouch. My hands are shaking so badly, I drop it on the ground, nearly scattering the various picks through the grass beside the door.

Get a grip, Nicky.

Aaron's voice floats through my head before I can stop it. I open the case and stare at the picks; it's been months since I've tried this. I haven't wanted to take them out, not since Aaron disappeared. In a way, it would have felt like a betrayal to use them without him.

"Not now, though," I say under my breath.

Because now I'm using them to help him. And maybe it's that reassurance that steadies my hands. I try the rake first, hoping I won't need any sort of torque. Of all houses, I would expect Aaron's to be nearly pick-proof. Strangely, though, the rake doesn't work, and I resort to the ball pick instead. It's such an easy choice, I wonder at first if that was by design, a sort of reverse psychology for the criminally minded.

Somehow, that thought doesn't comfort me as the front door to the Petersons' house opens a little too easily.

I run the garbage can back beside the driveway as planned before hurrying into the house and closing the door behind me, locking the secondary catch above the knob and barely noticing the crackling sound that follows the turn of the lock.

At first, I think nothing has changed. Through the entryway and the TV room I come to the kitchen. Oddly, the island that once stood in the center of the room is gone, replaced with a table and wooden chairs. But the big, gaping windows by the sink and hallway that leads to the bathroom are still in place.

Then I notice the smell. It's hard to believe it took this long to hit me; maybe fear has a way of delaying that sort of thing. But it's awful, like that summer Mom accidentally left a pound of ground beef in the car for three days. I spy the garbage can in the corner and see it's lined with a fresh bag. I think back to the garbage can near the driveway, to the months of garbage bags left on the curb by

Mr. Peterson. Whatever the smell is, it's not just laziness about taking out the trash.

I don't mean to, but I start to drift back toward the door, itching to retrace my steps back to a different hallway—to Mr. Peterson's office with its collage of photographs finding Aaron in every corner of the park, and to a basement I never did see.

I look into the dark TV room, to the boarded-up basement stairs, and I'm greeted by dark silence.

"Aaron?" I whisper. I know it's pointless. It has to be pointless. Of course he couldn't be down there.

I swallow. "Mya?" I say a little louder, and my breath quickens as I wait for an answer I know won't come. And yet . . .

A tap on the window behind me makes me leap back, and I have to lean against the kitchen counter to balance myself. I only have a second to find my breath, though, because I register it all at once: the pebble hitting the window, the flash of light as the sun reflects off of the windshield, Mr. Peterson's car rolling into the drive.

I look at my watch. 3:49 p.m. He isn't supposed to be home yet.

Move, stupid!

I turn left and right, but all I see are bare countertops. The space beside the phone where the flowered address book used to reside is empty.

I drop to the floor later than I should, but my brain isn't functioning right. Crawling on my hands and knees, I look for the first hiding place I can find, the mismatched double doors covering the wardrobe at the end of the hall. I dive through just in time to spring to my feet and ease the doors closed before I hear a car door swing open.

I hear Mr. Peterson emerge from the car, what sounds like grocery bags in hand, and then, nothing. I strain to listen for a few seconds, and that's as long as it takes for my stomach to drop to the floor because his footfalls tell me he's walking away from the front door and toward where Maritza is hiding. I listen for voices—the pleading explanations from Maritza, the menacing threats from Mr. Peterson. I don't hear voices, though. All I hear is the hair-raising screech of metal on concrete, the same sound I made when I hurried the trash can back to the side of the driveway. The screech lasts a second, just long enough to readjust it. Just like a person might straighten a picture that's gone crooked on a wall.

Footsteps approach, and with a jingle of keys, the lock turns, and Mr. Peterson is in the house.

He's taken a mere two steps inside before he stops, seemingly sniffing the air, but he doesn't gag like I did. I imagine him scanning the entryway slowly, searching for anything that might be out of place.

I've heard that some wild animals have attuned their

hearing to such an expert level that they can actually hear the blood pumping through their prey's body. I wasn't sure I believed it when I read it, but there's no doubt in my mind now. I wonder nervously if Mr. Peterson can smell me through the lingering stench of his house.

He turns to close the front door, but not before something catches his eye, and again, my stomach twists into a knot because I hear him crouching to inspect the catch on the door. I lean through the doors of the wardrobe and tiptoe down the hall to catch a glimpse of him reaching a finger to run along the inside of the frame, and I hear that same crinkle I dismissed upon locking the door behind me.

He peels away a clear film, and now I understand. Scotch tape. He didn't need to make the lock harder to pick. He just needed to know when someone had picked it.

And now he knows.

I lean into the shadows of the hall and race quietly back to the wardrobe as he lumbers into the kitchen. He places a paper sack on the kitchen counter and crouches to find the cutting board in a cupboard. Standing again, he walks slowly to the knife block and slides an extra-long carving knife from the wood, resting it carefully on the cutting board. Frighteningly fast, he upends the paper sack, letting an enormous lump of raw, bloody meat fall from its tissue wrapping. I gasp as it lands and slap my hand over my mouth, but Mr. Peterson only pauses for a second before he begins to hum a tune I swear I've heard before, an old nursery rhyme that makes the hairs on my forearms stand on end.

Slicing away the twine that binds the meat, Mr. Peterson raises his voice to hum louder, then, as though propelled by his deep baritone, lifts his arm high overhead, blade shining, before landing it deep in the raw flesh on the chopping block. He struggles to free the knife, then brings it up again, plunging it deeper still into the tissue.

I watch in horror as he doesn't prepare the meat on the block in front of him so much as he appears to mutilate it. I don't want to watch his eyes, but I can't help it. They glitter and glow in the reflection of the window each time he brings the knife up and back down, his mustache quivering under the humming that grows louder and louder in his throat, flaring his nostrils as he breaths the tune rather than sing it.

Except then he does start to sing.

> *"Tom, Tom, the piper's son,*
> *Stole a pig and away did run."*

He brings the knife high and lands it once more in the meat, leaving it this time to protrude from the mound, its handle half-buried.

Then he looks up, and I'd swear he looks straight through the bent slats, and impossibly, straight at me.

"The pig was eat, and Tom was beat,
And Tom went howling down the street."

The blood that should be flowing through my body has gotten trapped somewhere, I'm sure of it. My limbs freeze to icicles, and suddenly I can't feel my hands. They were covering my mouth, but who could tell anymore? The rhyme is old and folksy, and somehow I flash back to a schoolyard dance that went with it, something with streamers and a tall maypole, but none of that matters because Mr. Peterson isn't singing some sweet little folk song to pass the afternoon while cooking up a delicious meal.

He's singing a warning into the rank air of the house he knows isn't empty.

"Now," he says with so much menace in his voice, I am certain he's speaking directly to me. "Where did I put that salt?"

He smiles the most horrible smile I think I've ever seen before wiping his hands on a dirty dishrag and taking one step toward the wardrobe, then another, then another.

He reaches his hand to the doorknob and begins to pull.

The doorbell rings.

Mr. Peterson's hand pauses, then closes to a fist. He seems to wait for a moment to see if it will go away, only to drop his hand to his side when it rings twice more in quick succession.

He disappears around the corner, and I vaguely hear the front door open.

"You Mr. T. Peterson? Need you to sign for this."

I still can't feel my hands, but somehow they manage to nudge the wardrobe doors open, and I burst through like I'm on fire. I don't even care about making noise anymore. I have one chance to get out, and this is it.

I'm nearly to the bathroom door, when I spot it out of the corner of my eye: a cracked kitchen drawer under the phone, the shimmer of tiny flowers against a golden cover.

I rip the drawer open and yank the book from its resting place, forgetting to close it before running straight into the open drawer and knocking the wind out of me. I close it just as I hear the front door shut, but I don't turn back. I run into the bathroom off the kitchen and fling the window open, pulling it closed behind me just in time to dive beneath the window, back pressed close to the house's siding. I hear the sound of a delivery truck driving off, and I eye the high fence before me warily.

I haven't climbed a fence in a while, and I'm pretty sure I remember seeing a BEWARE OF DOG sign on the neighboring house's gate, but none of that slows me from clawing my way over that fence and then two more. I don't slow down until I've climbed in and out of every backyard until I reach the end of Friendly Court, stopping only to catch my breath and wipe the sweat from my forehead before it gets in my eyes.

"So much for your schedule."

I jump so far back I fall into a tangle of particularly pokey bushes.

Maritza extends her arm and pulls me out, even though she has to pull back with all her weight to get enough leverage.

"Eleven minutes early," I say, shaking my head. "Guess we should have listened to Trinity."

"Yeah," Maritza says, looking equally solemn, but then she smiles at me. "You can thank me later, by the way."

I start to get defensive, ready to show her the book I managed to snag. Then I remember what happened right before.

"Did you—?"

"Paid the American Parcel guy five bucks to ring the doorbell," she says, clearly proud of herself.

And I know I probably owe her my life, or at least a huge bowl of chocolate-covered bananas, but I can't let her steal all the glory.

I reach behind my back and pull the address book from my waistband and watch Maritza's eyes grow wide. Not only does all the feeling return to my hands, but suddenly it's like everything inside of me is electrified.

I fan the pages, then remember that we're still outside and probably far from safe.

"C'mon, let's go give Aunt Lisa a call."

We climb fences on the other side of the street this time, slipping into my house through the sliding door to the backyard. Back inside, I run to retrieve the phone from my dad's office while Maritza flips to the Ps.

"How do we know if her last name is still Peterson?" I ask, but Maritza's already reaching impatiently for the phone.

"Because it is."

She points to an L. Peterson, fourth on a list of five Peterson family phone numbers.

She starts to dial, when I remember a critical detail.

"Wait just a sec."

I sprint up the stairs and rummage through my desk drawers, coming up empty before remembering there's a

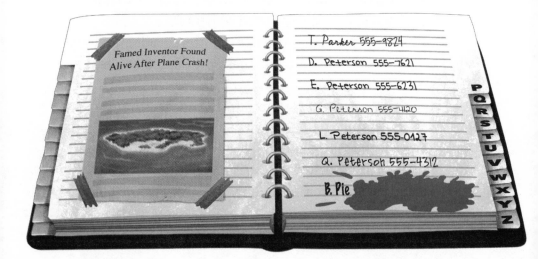

Famed Inventor Found
Alive After Plane Crash!

T. Parker 555-9824
D. Peterson 555-7621
E. Peterson 555-6231
G. Peterson 555-4120
L. Peterson 555-0127
Q. Peterson 555-4312
B. Pie

box in my closet that's become a resting place for all the parts I still haven't found a use for. I pull it down from the shelf and rummage through dismantled motors and keyboards before locating the brick-shaped device Dad passed down to me when he upgraded his audio recorder in September. He figured the old one was only good for parts, but he underestimated me. It works better than ever now.

Back downstairs, Maritza waits with her hand over the buttons, and when I nod, she dials the last four digits, then holds the phone far enough from her ear that we can both hear if we press our heads together.

A woman answers on the fourth ring.

"Hi, Aunt Li—? I mean, is this Lisa Peterson?"

The woman on the other end hesitates. "Whom may I ask is calling?"

"We're, uh, we're friends of Aaron and Mya," Maritza stumbles nervously. "From Raven Brooks."

The woman is silent.

"We're just wondering . . . um . . . may we please speak to them?"

The line is quiet, and at first I think maybe we've been disconnected.

Then the woman's voice changes from hesitation to something more like anger. "Well, why on earth would you be calling here looking for them? Doesn't their own father know where they are?"

Maritza and I exchange puzzled expressions. "It's just that Mr. Peterson said that he sent Aaron and Mya to live with you for a while, and we, um, just want to, you know, see how they're doing."

We wait another long second for her to respond, then another. Only this time, she doesn't say anything. This time, Aunt Lisa simply hangs up the phone.

Maritza and I stare at the receiver until the circuit's busy signal kicks on, and only then do I hit stop on the recorder.

"So, I guess it's real, then," Maritza says, and I'm glad she did because I can't seem to be the one to say it. "Mr. Peterson really is lying about where his kids are."

We keep staring at the phone like we expect it to give us more answers, but something tells me Aunt Lisa from Minnesota won't be picking up her phone for us again anytime soon.

Suddenly, a hot wave of anger washes over me at the thought of all these grown-ups who are willing to look the other way while Aaron and Mya are missing.

"Yeah," I say through gritted teeth as I grip the handheld recorder. "It's real. Only this time, we have proof that he's lying."

Chapter 11

The quad is full of kids who look just as thrilled to be back at school as we are. But while everyone else is already sick of required reading and solving for x, my stomach has been twisting all day with the thought of running into Enzo or explaining to Trinity how we got the recording of Aunt Lisa. Enzo has basketball tryouts today, though, and he managed to completely ignore me during the one class we have together.

Trinity is another story.

"You got what? And how? And are you nuts?"

"Aunt Lisa on tape saying she doesn't have Aaron and Mya. We finished the mission. And yes, we're nuts." Maritza says it all in one breath, saving me the effort.

"No, I mean you're seriously out of your minds. Do you have any idea what might have happened to you?" Trinity scolds.

I wince as I picture the glint of the blade of Mr. Peterson's knife as he drove it again and again into the meat on the cutting board.

"I have a pretty good idea, yes," I say.

Trinity takes a deep breath, and I wonder if she is equal parts exasperated and jealous that she wasn't with us when we finally got to talk to Aunt Lisa.

"We need more," Trinity says, and Maritza throws her hands in the air.

"Hello? Earth to Trinity! She just admitted Aaron and Mya aren't there!"

"Which means maybe Mr. Peterson lied to some gossipmonger about where they are. That doesn't mean he did something bad with them," Trinity says with her signature calm.

"Of course it does!" Maritza practically shouts.

As much as I hate to admit it, Trinity's right.

"Even if it proves he lied, so what?" I say reluctantly. "He could just make up another lie about where they 'really' are, and then we'd be right back where we are now."

"Except worse," Trinity adds. "Because now he knows we're onto him. He'll be more careful and less likely to drop a clue."

We're silent for a second before Trinity says, "We need more than proof that they *aren't* somewhere. We need proof of where they actually *are*."

I think back to my dreams, to the mannequin's hand rising from the dirt. To my own late-night digging in the shadow of the Rotten Core. "The park," I say before I know I'm doing it.

To my surprise, Trinity shakes her head. "We're too late. That's part of what the town hall was about last night.

The EarthPro people have fenced it off and set up security cameras."

The air leaves my body. "Just like the factory."

"Right. And they're going to have one more town hall tomorrow night. That'll be the final vote."

"So much for a ninety-day waiting period. They're going to tear up the park," Maritza says, shaking her head.

"Which means we need to find out what he's hiding there before they do," I say.

"We'll double our efforts," Trinity says. "Watch him twenty-four seven if we have to."

Maritza nods. "Remember, we need proof. Who has a camera?"

They both turn to me.

"Don't look at me."

"How can you of all people not have a camera?" Maritza asks.

I shrug. "It's on my list."

Then she turns to Trinity.

"No way. My dad just got it for her. They'd kill me!"

Maritza fills me in. "He got it for her mom's birthday. It's really nice, with a zoom lens and everything."

"To bring to *Uganda* this summer," Trinity says. "To document *sorghum farms*, not for spying on the neighbor! Seriously, no. It's impossible. Besides, she'd know if it went missing."

"For a night?" Maritza persists. "Besides, didn't you say your parents work late all the time these days?"

I know I should help Trinity out, but we really do need that camera. "We'll be super careful," I say, and I know by the way her shoulders fall that Trinity's giving in.

"We'll meet at seven at Nicky's. Come in through the backyard just in case," Maritza orders, and we nod.

* * *

At home that night, dinner is a mostly silent affair while we each stew in our own thoughts. Dad's preoccupied with his meeting at work tonight with Mr. Esposito and Mrs. Yi, no doubt a play for winning Dad over to their side and writing the story that will seal the deal on swaying the town toward the EarthPro development. Mom is irritated with me, though. It's Science Alliance Night at her work, and apparently, sometime during my social embargo over winter break, I agreed to go with her so she could show me why I should consider getting involved in the Young Biologists Club.

"I'm sorry, Mom. Really, I am. It's just that Trin and Maritza are counting on me, and I can't just back out at the last minute."

"But you can back out of your commitment to me at the last minute," Mom says, and I know that's hurt in her voice, but what can I do? The only way to make her understand is

Science Alliance Night!
7 P.M. - 8 P.M.

Meet and greet scientists from Raven Brooks and hear all about their research!

Refreshments to be served.
Don't forget your thinking cap!

to tell her what I'm actually doing tonight, and that's out of the question, so I'm finding every way to avoid saying it.

"You know, it's not that I want you to be a scientist," she says a little defensively.

I lift an eyebrow.

"Okay, it would be great, I admit it. I'd finally have someone to talk molecules with," she says, and now it's Dad's turn to get defensive.

"I talk molecules with you!" he says, pouting.

Mom rolls her eyes skyward. "My point is, you don't have to be a scientist or a journalist or a parent or whatever. All we're asking is that you be *something*."

I stare at my plate. I'm so many things, but I'm not sure any of them would make my mom and dad proud.

"We need to see some evidence that you're exploring your interests," Dad says through a bite of his snack cake, sounding strangely more like Mom than Mom is in this moment. I wonder if they decided to trade approaches to throw me off.

"Like tonight," Mom says, piling on. "What's so important that you can't at least give science a chance?" she asks, like science is the equivalent of some gross-looking vegetable I have to try before I get dessert.

And finally, inspiration strikes. "Photography," I say. "We're meeting up with Trinity to check out her mom's new camera. She photographs things all over the world."

Mom's face lights up, and though he tries to hide it, Dad's smile is impossible to miss.

And the best part is it's not even a lie.

"Photography," Mom repeats, eating the rest of her dinner in happier silence.

I nod. *Dear Aliens, please don't vaporize me for telling only half the truth.*

When I make it through all of dinner with my molecules still intact, I breathe a deep sigh and wave my parents down the driveway, then disappear into the house and wait by the back door for Trinity and Maritza.

* * *

It really is a nice camera. It took me five minutes to convince Trinity to let me hold it, and once I proved I at least sort of knew what I was doing with the various buttons and zooms, she let me test it out from my bedroom window. The range was stronger and sharper than my binocuscope, and of course had the added bonus of being able to capture pictures—actual proof of Mr. Peterson's activities.

"Now we just need to catch him in the act of doing . . . something," Maritza sighs, saying what we're all thinking. I turn to my daily schedule in my binder and confirm what I already remembered: Thursday nights from seven to nine are marked as *VARIABLE*. Meaning sometimes he goes out, sometimes he doesn't.

As if on cue, a creak from outside makes the three of us turn and duck in unison. Mr. Peterson steps cautiously through the front door, walking toward his car. Instead of getting into his car, he walks to the backyard and returns to the driveway rolling the same wheelbarrow he had with him the last time he went to the Golden Apple Amusement Park, when he almost caught Maritza and me running away.

This time, though, there's something in the wheelbarrow.

"Is that a—?" Trinity breathes as she peers over the windowsill from our crouched positions.

"A shovel," I finish. I see Maritza's grip on her backpack tighten.

He's out of the driveway and halfway down the street before it occurs to any of us to move.

"C'mon, before we lose him!" Trinity hisses, and we're out the back door and hopping fences as quietly as we can, keeping Mr. Peterson in our sights each time we reach the top of another fence. Trinity slings her mom's camera around her neck and pins the strap under one arm to keep it from jostling.

Sure enough, Mr. Peterson heads for the woods and cuts a path that's become all too familiar to me, and probably Maritza, too. Trinity doesn't say anything as she leads the way, ducking behind overgrowth every time we dare to move, then signaling to Maritza and me when the coast is clear, always careful to keep a safe distance from Mr. Peterson. Thankfully, the shovel rolling around in the metal wheelbarrow clangs around enough to cover any sounds our crunching feet and huffing breath might make.

At last, we reach the old entrance to Golden Apple Amusement Park, with its charred sign and graffiti-smeared directory map, vines choking the twisted and rusted metal of whatever remains. The fencing has started to go up around the park, but it's incomplete around the back half— just rolled fencing lying on the ground every forty feet or so.

Mr. Peterson is on a mission, heading straight toward that part of the park, exactly in the direction of the Rotten Core roller coaster.

Exactly in the direction of where I woke up on a night

that feels like forever ago, digging through the dirt for something I'm now terrified might actually be there.

Maritza signals to the last place we took cover when we caught Mr. Peterson ransacking the park. When we arrive at the overgrowth, we keep low and watch as he once again begins filling his wheelbarrow with various machine parts, yanking wires from roller coaster cars and running to different parts of the park to retrieve the debris of his destroyed creation. He's set the shovel against the trunk of a nearby tree, and the spade of it glows unsettlingly against the pale light of the moon.

Mr. Peterson is panting; I can hear it from here. Little

beads of sweat begin to form on his brow, shimmering under the same silver moonlight that sets the shovel aglow. I've completely forgotten about the pictures until the tiniest click makes me flinch, and the three of us freeze as Mr. Peterson stands erect, his hands full of parts, surveying the trees before returning to his work.

We all breathe, and I nod at Trinity to keep going. She clicks away, no longer catching Mr. Peterson's attention. He must think it's some sort of woodland creature doing its nighttime work. All is going according to plan so far, but it's not lost on me that we still need more. So far, we've caught him stealing garbage. Hardly the crime of the century. And certainly not proof of anything having to do with the whereabouts of Aaron and Mya.

Then he starts to hum. It's the same horrible song he sang while I hid in his house—all about that kid who stole something and was beaten for it—and for a second I think he must know we're here, but he's still moving garbage, still filling his wheelbarrow, still unaware of the camera clicks.

Then, when he's filled his wheelbarrow to the brim, he turns to the shovel, wipes the sweat from his brow, and begins to dig. I do a double take as I realize it actually *is* the same spot where I was digging in my sleep, and while my suspicion is confirmed, I feel zero gratification. Nothing would make me happier than to realize we've just been taking pictures of some dude losing his mind, Aaron and Mya are simply staying with a different relative, and I don't "wander" so much as randomly sleepwalk. It's still possible this could all be a huge misunderstanding, just a strange coincidence.

Right?

Then Mr. Peterson drops to his hands and knees in the dirt he's just unearthed and balls his fists in the muck, bringing up chunks when he raises his hands to his face and squeezes his head hard, streaking dark dirt across his temples and letting the dirt pile on top of his shoulders. His face goes a deep purple under the moonlight that's begun to cloud over, and then his hands form fists again, and he begins to beat the sides of his head.

"Stupid, stupid, *stupid*! I couldn't stop it. Why couldn't I stop it?"

Trinity clicks behind me once or twice, then stops, and we all stare in horrified fascination as Mr. Peterson comes apart.

"They'll never believe me. They'll never believe. But I had to. Don't they understand I had to?"

I can't tell which of us is shaking, but it's starting to rattle the dead leaves underfoot, and I hold my hand to steady the trembling leg I think is Maritza's.

Mr. Peterson lets go of his head. "My little angel, forgive me."

Then he thrusts his shovel into the dirt and reaches into the hole he's made.

What he holds in his hand is long and pale under the newly uncovered moon.

It all happens too fast. Maritza gasps and brings her hand quickly to her mouth, nudging Trinity's elbow in the process, which must accidentally flip a switch on the fancy camera, making Trinity's next picture produce the brightest, most blinding flash of light I've ever seen.

Silence pours over us in a wave, heavy and suffocating. Then someone is pulling me to my feet, and someone else is yelling at me to run.

"C'mon, c'mon!" she yells, and I can hear it's Trinity.

"No, this way!" a different voice yells, and that's Maritza, but if not for someone holding my hand, whipping me past the trees and across narrow wooded paths, I would be lost because I still can't see anything but white.

"Oh my God. Oh my God."

"Freak out later, Mari!"

"Oh my God, it's true. It's true."

"Mari!"

"In here!"

They pull me into someplace dark and enclosed that smells like freshly cut grass and manure. In this new dark place, my vision starts to return, just in time to see through a crack in the door of what appears to be someone's gardening shed on the outskirts of town bordering the woods.

Just in time to see Mr. Peterson emerge, shovel in hand, dragging the spade over the asphalt with menace.

"Tom, Tom, the piper's son," he sings, and Maritza squeezes my hand hard enough to make my knuckles crack.

"Stole a pig and away did run." Trinity shakes her head slowly, as though willing him not to look this way. It doesn't work, though. After a cursory survey of the road, he zeros in on the very shed where we're huddled, fingers laced and breath shared.

"The pig was eat, and Tom was beat." He takes a step closer, dragging his shovel and humming his horrible song.

"And Tom went howling down the street," he finishes, and a deep, burbling laugh rumbles from his lips.

He takes a step closer, then another, and with his hand on the handle of the shed door, I know that our time is up. We came so close, but we failed. We failed one another and we failed Aaron and Mya. I failed my parents by lying, by never realizing my potential, by never talking molecules with my mom and never telling my dad it wasn't his fault that jobs went away.

I brace myself for the end.

Then I hear something . . . burp?

Mr. Peterson turns, then squints into the distance. Soon his eyes are wide as I hear footsteps approach.

I hear another burp. Then another, and a grunt or sneeze of some kind.

"Frank Beauregard Tuttle, what in the name of David are

you doing all the way out there? Margaret Adelaide, you know better! Get your wooly behinds back here this instant!"

Maritza's grip on my hand begins to loosen. Trinity's hand moves from my arm to her mouth as she hides a nervous snort. I look up to a familiar sight above me, and I can't tell if it's the Aliens or Aaron watching over me.

"Hey, who's there?" Farmer Llama yells from a distance, and I see Mr. Peterson through the crack in the door start to back away, picking up his shovel so it stops dragging.

"This is private property!" Farmer Llama threatens. "I'll call the cops!"

Mr. Peterson gives one more ferocious glance toward the shed door we hide behind before turning and disappearing from sight.

Once Farmer Llama's footsteps finally approach, I've let

go of Maritza's hand completely, opting to brace myself against the riding lawn mower. Farmer Llama wrangles his precious llamas while we sweat, his gruffness softening as he realizes their heroism.

"Well, look at you two," he says admiringly. "I think you earned yourself the good stuff tonight. Papa's gonna fix you each a whole sweet potato."

One of them sneezes.

"You catchin' a cold, Maggie?"

He walks them away, their grunts and grumbles growing softer as they return to their barn for a hero's feast. If I could, I'd feed them a truckload of sweet potatoes.

That night, after Trinity pinkie-swears to drop off the roll of film the second the Photo Mat opens tomorrow, I lie in bed trying not to think of what Maritza said to me after we walked Trinity back to her house. There's no chance she's right, so I might as well just forget she said anything at all.

But I know there's more than a chance she's right. After all we've seen, after all our suspicions have panned out, of course there's a chance it's true.

No matter how many pillows I pile on top of my head, I can't muffle the sound of her voice telling me just what it was that made her jump, knocking the camera's flash and setting off our harrowing escape.

"It was a body, Nicky. That was someone's arm he pulled from the dirt."

Chapter 12

I had zero chance of sleeping last night, but somehow, awareness of that fact does nothing to soothe the aching fatigue and scratchy feeling on my eyes every time my lids close over them. Not that I really wanted to go to sleep. Who knows where I'd end up, and barricading myself in my room would be pretty difficult to explain to my parents without admitting all the times I'd accidentally left the house in the middle of the night.

That was someone's arm he pulled from the dirt.

I can't unhear the sound of Maritza's voice, the way her throat seemed to close over the words that must have been almost impossible for her to say.

"Earth to young Mr. Roth," I hear Mr. Pierce say, and I blink hard to try to break my trance, but he's still blurry, standing up there in front of the whiteboard pointing to a partially diagrammed sentence.

"What?"

"I said, can you identify the dangling modifier?" Mr. Pierce says like it's the most important question.

Seth cackles at the front of the room. "Dude, if your modifier's dangling, you should blow your nose. That's sick."

Ruben punches Seth's shoulder, rolling a basketball back and forth between his legs. It's the first time I notice that Enzo isn't sitting in the seat beside Ruben. He's all the way on the other end of the room. Instead, there's some supertall, skinny kid I've never seen before sitting in his usual place, and he's laughing right along with Seth and Ruben.

"Unlike you, I'd rather it come out of my nose than get lodged in my throat," I say before I realize I'm saying it. I'm too tired to care, though.

"That's enough, all of you," Mr. Pierce says, but he's already lost the class.

"Gross, you swallowed a loogie?" some girl says, scooting her desk away from Seth.

"I didn't swallow it!"

"He just misfired," Ruben tries to defend his friend, but now the new kid next to him is scooting his desk away, too.

"Mr. Pierce, can we please stop talking about loogies? I have a very sensitive stomach," a girl calls from behind me.

"You've gotta start at the back of your throat," someone else offers. "It's all about projection."

"I'm gonna puke."

And so it went for the remaining ten minutes of class, which felt like ten years. But I stopped listening once I realized Enzo wasn't listening, either. Instead, he stared at something near the floor at the front of the room. When the bell rang, I tried to make my way over to him, but I was too slow and he was the first one out the door. Maybe if I'd been more awake, I would have put it together, but it took passing by the gym before I understood.

There on the metal door leading to the basketball courts was a typed list of names divided into two columns under *Starters* and *Substitutes*. Enzo's name isn't on either list.

I consider calling him when I get home, but the minute

Raven Brooks Middle School Boys Basketball Team

Starters

Collin Jones

Seth Jenkins

Ruben Smith

James Kinsman

Jake Louis

Substitutes

David Miles

Michael Gonzalez

Christopher Park

Matthew Wheelahan

Travis Coleman

Josh Brown

Tyler Wray

I reach my room, all I manage to do is fall into bed. I only wake up when my parents come to retrieve me.

"Time for fun," Dad says, and it's a whopper of a lie.

* * *

It was supposed to rain tonight, but instead, a light snow is blanketing the town. And it's freezing. At long last, winter is in full swing. I'd say better late than never, but never would have been fine by me. You'd think the weather would have been reason enough to cancel the town hall, but it appears nothing—not rain nor bone-chilling frost nor dinnertime conflicts or plain human decency appear to be enough to keep the people of Raven Brooks from shouting at one another across the aisle in the middle of the Square.

And maybe that's best. Maybe we just need to get it over with. Apparently, the town hall from two days ago was far from civil—hence the *final* town hall, where we'll make a decision and get on with it.

"Let's just throw a mud pit in the middle and have everyone take a turn," Mom says as we pile out of the car, and for maybe the first time ever, Dad is the one throwing *her* the disapproving look.

"What? You know I'm right. You're just sorry you weren't the one to say it," she says, and Dad smiles for the first time all day.

Then she stops him by the back of the car and pulls him close. "Miguel is your friend. Not just your boss. Your *friend*. He'll see reason, and you'll see the end of this. After tonight, the city will decide what to do, and we'll move on from this whole ordeal."

"It's all just such a big mess," Dad says, and Mom says what she says in the face of any huge mess:

"Meh. Grab a sponge."

There's comfort in that thought, the idea of wetting a rag and wiping away all this contention, scrubbing away the misery that the oblivious people of EarthPro have dredged up, the grief Mrs. Yi buried too shallowly, the conclusions the people of Raven Brooks didn't know they'd formed after Lucy died. Is it possible one good swipe of vinegar could clean all that agony away?

"If everyone would please take a seat," a woman in an uncomfortable-looking red pea coat says into the microphone.

"They have audio," a familiar voice says behind me. "So you know they're serious."

I turn to see Enzo standing a little ways behind me. The first thing I notice is his hair, and I swear to the Aliens I've never been so relieved to see his mercifully floppy hair. I can't see even an ounce of gel in there.

Somewhere inside of me, a pin that's been holding my whole body rigid falls away, and I feel like every joint is loosened. My shoulders fall, and the burning at the back of my neck cools to a simmer before the flame goes out altogether.

"Hey, what's up?" is what I manage to say, and I slap the hand he's extended to me like nothing has happened over the past couple of months.

"You, uh, you come with friends, or—?" I say because maybe all the tension hasn't left just yet. Maybe there's still a little bit of it inside of me.

Enzo looks down, smiling sheepishly. "Nah, I'm meeting Trinity here. My dad wanted me to ride with him," he says.

It's what he doesn't say that I notice more, though. Not a word about basketball or Seth or Ruben. Not a word about the roster that didn't have his name on it, or the seat in English class that wasn't saved for him, or the gel that isn't in his hair.

The crowds have begun to gather, and people are starting to shuffle toward their chairs.

"See you afterward?" he says.

I nod, and I see the anxiety dissipate in Enzo, too.

Just as he turns toward the row of chairs where his dad waits, I punch his shoulder.

"I should have tried out," I say, surprising myself a little. "I mean, I should have tried *something*."

I surprise Enzo, too. I know he doesn't quite understand, though.

"I mean, you had the guts to try out . . ." I add, and I think he gets it that time. I think he knows that he was braver than me.

Then he shrugs and borrows an expression from my mom: "Meh."

He shifts his weight from one foot to the other.

"I shouldn't have, you know, said what I said. At the party. I was being stupid. I just, I don't know. I wanted to be—"

"Not a freak?"

Enzo smiles sheepishly. "You aren't a freak." Then he stops smiling and turns serious. "Neither is Aaron."

And that's the end of it—of basketball and missed Taco Shack meet-ups and unreturned calls. It's not the end of balls of paper flicked at the backs of jerks' heads in his defense. I'll always do that. This time, though, I have a little more confidence that Enzo would do the same for me.

RAVEN BROOKS TOWN HALL: EARTHPRO DEVELOPMENT

OPEN FLOOR DEBATE AND SPECIAL ELECTION

Moderator: Councilwoman Jane Barinski, Raven Brooks Development Committee

Speakers: Brenda Yi, Marcia Tillman

"People, we're about to start," says the woman in the tight red suit. She looks tired, like she still has to make tomorrow's lunches for her kids when she gets home.

Feedback from the amplifier makes the microphone squawk, and that seems to be enough to capture everyone's attention long enough to stop talking. Most are in seats now, flimsy folding chairs set in rows in the middle of the Square, in front of the dancing apple fountain that they drain in the winter. More people keep showing up, though, and now they're piling in behind the chairs, looming over the people seated.

"Thank you all for joining us tonight," says the lady in the red suit. "For those of you I haven't met . . . I'm sure there are still a few of you"—some kind chuckles ripple the crowd—"I'm Councilwoman Jane Barinski, and I oversee the development committee. I have to say, I never thought this was going to be such an exciting gig."

She doesn't look excited.

"Right, so let's get on with it. I understand we have a designated speaker for each side before we hold our special election. Have we decided who will be going first?" Councilwoman Barinski asks no one in particular.

"I'll go first," says a voice I couldn't possibly forget.

Mrs. Tillman ascends the steps onto the small stage, gathering the tiers of her flowy tie-dyed skirt, beads dangling from the drawstring at the waist, exposing thick wool tights and sandals with socks underneath. A hush falls over the crowd.

Actually, that's not true. It's not all hushed. There is a low ripple of something like grumbling on one side of the crowd that is divided right down the middle like a courtroom. And on the other side of the aisle is a cluster of stony-faced men and women staring down the grumblers, clearly unhappy with the low-grade heckling of their spokesperson.

"Ladies and gentlemen of Raven Brooks," Mrs. Tillman begins, a velvety sort of overlay atop the abrasive cadence of her voice. "I thank you all for coming out this evening for such a crucial vote. You truly are the ray of light that shines upon the lotus petal."

Smatterings of applause follow, but people mostly turn to one another in confusion.

"It is your radiance, your essence, and the core of your being that allows Raven Brooks to transcend the ordinary and break down the barriers of human limitations."

A touch less applause this time, but Mrs. Tillman doesn't seem to notice. She closes her eyes and holds a fist to her heart.

"And it is your higher truth, your enlightened spirit, that I call on now as we embrace each other in mind, body and soul . . ."

Mrs. Tillman's speech has thoroughly confused even

her supporters, and it's clear they've begun to regret their choice of spokesperson. People are starting to breathe into their hands to warm them.

Ms. McGraw, who runs the Gamers Grotto, finally stands. "We want you to vote against these EarthPro people because they're gonna put us all out of business!"

Mrs. Tillman opens her eyes and drops her hands to her sides. "That's exactly what I'm saying."

"Someone tell that Grape-Nut that EarthPro builds houses, not wackadoodle health food stores!"

"I think we can keep the name-calling to a minimum, Mr. Picune," Councilwoman Barinski says from the edge of the stage.

"It starts with homes, and then come the big-box stores!" yells someone else, and she receives a round of applause from the anti-EarthPro side.

"Oh yes, heaven forbid we'd have a *choice* about where to shop!" someone else yells, earning a round of applause from the pro-development side of the aisle.

"People! People! This is exactly what we said we were going to avoid tonight!" the councilwoman yells to the sky, and I bet there's nothing she'd rather be doing more right now than eating peanut butter out of the jar with a spoon and watching old *Perry Mason* episodes on the Classics channel.

"Still looking for that mud pit," I hear Mom say from somewhere behind me.

Then, out of nowhere, a hush falls over the crowd, a real one this time. It takes a second, but I finally see the source of the calm as she climbs the steps to the stage, displacing Mrs. Tillman and lowering the microphone to mouth level.

Brenda Yi is dressed in jeans and a button-down white shirt underneath her puffy coat. Her hair is pulled into a neat ponytail, and she's every bit as measured and controlled as she was at the *Banner* holiday party. There's a storm behind that ironed shirt and smoothed hair, though. If I were close enough to her, I would be able to see it in her eyes, I'm certain of it. I would see the rolling clouds and the streaks of lightning. I would see a person who is still standing, but an incomplete person with a crucial piece missing, something the storm washed away forever.

"Thank you for listening to me," Brenda Yi says, as though anyone would dare not to. "I know this has been a difficult winter."

She waits to see if anyone will disagree. No one does.

"Raven Brooks is unlike any town I've ever visited, unlike any other I've even heard of. It is . . . special."

There are murmurs of agreement.

"It's that specialness that made my husband and I decide to buy a home and start a family here so many years ago."

Utter silence.

"And when I lost my family—" Brenda Yi swallows,

then takes a deep breath. "When I lost my family, it was this very special town that helped bring me back to life."

An old woman sniffles in the corner by the fountain, and her husband wraps an arm around her shoulders.

"I would never dream of allowing anyone to rob our beautiful community of that specialness. Truly, I wouldn't. But throughout this protracted and painful argument of whether or not to develop the land where the old Golden Apple properties sit, there's been a perspective missing, and I'd like to offer that perspective to you now. Not to make anyone feel guilty, or to sway your decision against your own conscience, but to help you understand why I want EarthPro to build their homes.

"It's not because I'm eager to see a new corporation develop the land we hold so dear. In all honesty, I don't like that idea at all. Of course I'm worried about the fate of our independent businesses. But I still fully intend to patronize those businesses and *only* those businesses, and I hope that you'll all make a similar promise."

Brenda Yi takes another deep breath.

"I want EarthPro to develop because I want them to make something new and wonderful where there is still something old and ugly. I want them to scrape away the last of what haunts the outskirts of Raven Brooks and help us finally, *finally*, start fresh. Start new. Start over."

Her eyes fill with tears.

"I'm asking you to please remember my daughter. I think you all do. I don't doubt that she left an impression on many hearts in this crowd today. But keeping the ruins alive of a nightmare just makes it so that we can never really wake up."

She wipes her eyes.

"And I want desperately to wake up."

We don't clap. We don't say a word. Brenda Yi leaves the stage and joins a small group of people she allows to hold her and cover her from the audience while she wipes her eyes and blows her nose and smooths the stray hairs from her forehead.

And then the adults of Raven Brooks vote. They stand single-file in lines before makeshift booths, checking a single box on paper ballots and folding them into locked wooden boxes guarded by volunteers like Trinity's parents. I stand with Enzo and Maritza and Trinity as we watch them inch forward toward the booths, then toward the fold-ing tables, then toward the parking lot. Everyone's done talking. A few people shake hands or hug; a few smile and bow their heads toward neighbors they had fought with less than an hour ago.

I stand beside Enzo, a rush of relief at having made amends, but a new fear brewing in my belly because every-thing Brenda Yi said made so much sense, and if I had to guess, I'd bet she changed minds tonight. I'd bet she changed enough minds to let the EarthPro bulldozers dig up the land that used to belong to the Golden Apple Corporation.

Which means, unless we take our case to my dad or Enzo's dad in the next few days, any chance of finding evidence in the park could be sliding through our fingers with every cast of the ballot.

Enzo jabs an elbow into my waist. "Looks like your dad and my dad finally stopped acting like—"

"Like you two," Maritza says, watching the same reconciliation happen across the Square. All I can focus on is the way Mr. Esposito keeps patting my dad on the shoulder and the way Dad keeps smiling that weird smile he uses whenever he's pretending to agree with someone just to be polite.

When we get back to the car, Mom lets out a loud groan. "Can we please go out for ice cream now?" she whines, and it's so unlike her, Dad immediately turns the car into the drive-through of the Soft Serve. Three swirly cones later, Dad's struggling to steer one-handed, and I'm trying to think of all the ways I can subtly broach the topic of Mr. Peterson with my dad. The photos should be developed tomorrow, and now with the vote coming out in the morning, we'll need to move fast.

We pull into the driveway a few minutes later. Mom is so singularly focused on her cone, she barely notices us hanging back while she heads inside.

"So that's it?" I ask my dad. "You're going to write in favor of clearing the land?"

"I don't see what it would matter at this point," Dad says, licking a drip of ice cream from his cone. "It seemed pretty clear that Brenda swayed most everyone in the crowd to her side. The vote'll come out in the morning in favor of tearing down the park. Democracy won in the end. As a journalist, I have to accept and report that."

"I understand," I say. "I've . . . kind of been doing some reporting of my own."

"Not of . . ." He nods his head across the street. "Right?"

I drop my gaze. Maybe this was not the right time to ease Dad into this.

"Narf, I thought I told you to leave that alone."

"Dad, I—"

"I know I don't play the dad card with you often. You're a good kid, a smart kid, and I like to think that's because I had something to do with it."

"Dad, it's just—I followed him to the park, and he was up to something," I say, skating on the thinnest ice I've ever attempted. I guess this is what people mean when they talk about desperate times and desperate measures.

Dad's face is suddenly red enough for me to see even in the dark of the driveway. "You . . . *followed* him?" He lowers his voice, putting his arm around me and leading me up to the door. "Nicky, this is invasive. This is not okay. When we talked about this, I thought you understood."

"He dug up a—"

"Listen, I know we let you off the hook a little easy about the audio incident, but that was just a prank. This is *stalking*. Do you understand me, Nicholas?"

Nicholas. So, there we have it. My first real fight with Dad.

I want to put up more of a struggle, partly because this is more serious than Dad understands, and partly because, if this is the beginning of my teenaged rebellious streak, I might as well go all the way with it. But neither of us seems to have the stomach. I'm feeling that same stab of parental disappointment I did from the audio incident, even though in this one shining moment, I *know* I'm right. But Dad's so mad, he dumps his ice cream cone right into the garbage can, wiping the drippings on his jeans.

"We're going to discuss this with your mom tomorrow," he says, turning off the porch light. "And you owe Mr. Peterson an apology."

Dad has no idea how much that thought freezes me in fear.

Chapter 13

"We caught everything," Trinity says the next day, her eyes impossibly wide.

"Like, everything," Maritza says, just in case I didn't catch the importance.

"I still can't believe you guys followed him into the woods. You're crazier than he is," Enzo says, but unlike my dad, he's not mad or disapproving. I think he's actually impressed.

"I plead temporary insanity," I say, leafing through the pictures of Mr. Peterson's clandestine activities, careful not to smudge the prints Trinity picked up right as the Photo Mat opened this morning.

The girls are right. Trinity captured every single one of Mr. Peterson's odd movements, frame by frame. There's Mr. Peterson putting wires and gears into his rusty old wheelbarrow. There he is digging. Then I come to the picture of Mr. Peterson seeing the blinding flash, his face frozen in a grimace that should be terrifying. After all, I'm nearly positive he would have buried us if he hadn't been run off by llamas. Still, there's something in his face, that frozen second of unguarded emotion.

He looks . . . sad.

Then I look closer at the picture to the mound of dirt unearthed behind him, the hole he'd so industriously dug while he didn't know he was being watched. There, a little blurry and out of focus, is the long, slim, pale form of what could easily be the arm Maritza swears she saw.

I let Enzo take the pictures from my hand to have a closer look.

"We have enough," Maritza says, and it seems like she's midthought when she says it, but we all know exactly what she means.

Trinity nods, counting off the proof, one bit of evidence on each finger. "There are the pictures," she says. "And Aunt Lisa accidentally admitting that Aaron and Mya aren't really with her."

"There's the food garbage, the TV dinners for more than one person," Maritza says, and I start to object, but she interrupts me. "It's not enough on its own, but it all adds to the bigger picture now. And there's the smell in his house."

"He could just be gross," Enzo says, and I have to agree.

"It's just like Trinity said—circumstantial evidence! Except now we've got real evidence, too," Maritza says.

"Like the note," Enzo says, looking at me.

I'd forgotten I even told him about it. The note Aaron left me, with the blood on it.

I nod. "Yeah. There's the note."

"We've got to go to the adults," Trinity says, as though she's referring to some holy council of sages instead of dopey Officer Keith, who's on Mrs. Tillman's speed dial at the natural grocer.

"We should tell Nicky's dad," Maritza says, and I go rigid.

"Yeah," Trinity says. "He's been super-fair about all the stories he writes in the paper about the whole situation. My parents keep calling your dad a *real newsman*, whatever that means," Trinity says, and I can't change the subject fast enough.

"We're . . . not on the best terms," I say, borrowing a phrase from none other than my dad. And I feel horrible saying it, like I didn't just let my dad down, I let my friends down, too.

"Then my dad," Enzo says, and I want to hug him for moving on so quickly.

We march to the Esposito house first thing after school, binder and photos and cassette tape in hand.

Enzo and Maritza's dad is halfway up a ladder in the front of their house, scooping dead leaves from the gutters and dropping them to the ground in heavy splats.

"It's important," Maritza says to their dad's questioning look. He doesn't ask a follow-up question. He didn't even ask a first question. It seems Mr. Esposito and his kids have a code about conversations that are worth climbing down ladders for. Seeing that sort of understanding in action makes me want to run home and tell my dad I'm sorry.

But there will be time for that later. Right now, Mr. Esposito knows that we all need lemonade.

Five glasses on the table, Mr. Esposito removes his heavy work gloves and sets them by the kitchen sink before easing into the wooden chair at the head of the table.

"Okay," he says after taking a long drink of his lemonade. "I'm ready."

Trinity and I look at each other, quietly realizing that we never discussed how we'd start, but it turns out, we didn't really need to. Maritza and Enzo have this part handled.

"Aaron and Mya Peterson aren't in Minnesota," Enzo starts, and the four of us wait for Mr. Esposito to react.

I'm not sure what I was expecting him to do—laugh or scold or walk away or argue—but I wasn't expecting him to believe us, that's for sure. That's why I'm so glad Maritza and Enzo know what to do when he finally says, "Keep talking."

"We called their aunt Lisa," Maritza says. "The one who was at Mrs. Peterson's funeral. She didn't mean to, but she admitted that they weren't with her."

Mr. Esposito stares hard at Maritza, and she looks down at the cassette tape in her hands, maybe because she knows that he's probably guessed she didn't get Aunt Lisa's phone number by just asking for it.

"And Mr. Peterson, he's been acting strange," Enzo says, pulling his dad's attention from his sister.

Mr. Esposito lifts an eyebrow at Enzo.

"Stranger than usual," Enzo clarifies.

"We have pictures," Trinity adds, and she places them in a neat pile at the center of the table.

We all stare at the glossy stack of four-by-six photos,

the picture on top a clear profile of Mr. Peterson piling machine parts into a wheelbarrow in the Golden Apple Amusement Park.

Mr. Esposito reaches slowly for the photos, and at a pace slow enough to make me want to scream, he examines each one, flipping it to the back of the stack before studying the next one. When he reaches the last picture in the stack, he starts over, puzzling over each and every detail of the photographs before setting them down on the table in front of him.

"Is there more?" he asks, and his tone is impossible to read.

"Nicky has a journal. He's been . . . surveilling him," Enzo says, and I thank him silently for avoiding the words "spying" or "stalking."

"And a note from Aaron," I say.

Mr. Esposito meets my eyes. "A note?"

"From right before he disappeared. There's . . . blood."

I carefully unfold the very last note I received from Aaron—the one that lodged in his broken window, floating down to the street.

Mr. Esposito takes the note carefully, holding my gaze long enough to make me understand he'll be careful with it.

He studies that one note for longer than he examined the entire stack of pictures.

It takes him so long to speak, I'm ready for him to do

almost anything: yell at us for being so reckless, laugh at us for being kids with too much time on their hands, tell us our case is pathetic.

Instead, he says, "From this point forward, you kids are to stay away from Mr. Peterson, do you understand?"

Frost shoots through my veins because Mr. Esposito is deadly serious.

"Don't follow him, don't talk to him, stay away from his house."

All heads turn to me.

"Stay as far away from his house as you can," Mr. Esposito corrects himself.

"We weren't trying to—" Maritza starts to defend us, but Mr. Esposito shows her his palm, and she immediately stops talking.

"I know, and I don't need to hear more about that," he says, and I think we all exhale one collective sigh. "This is troubling, though. What you've uncovered, whatever this is . . ." He points to the pictures, but then his gaze falls to the note from Aaron. "Whatever it is, it's more than we can handle."

Then he looks up, meeting our eyes, each of us, one at a time. "It's more than we *should* handle."

Mr. Esposito lifts the binder cover to close it over the pages, when something falls from the pocket and clatters to the table. He lifts it gingerly, the tiny apple charm dangling from his thick fingers. I watch his eyes closely, and a flicker of recognition passes over them.

He looks at Maritza.

"This is like yours," he says, his voice very quiet, like it's just a conversation between the two of them now.

Maritza nods.

"That one was Lucy's. We think Mya had it, but she left it for Nicky to find. We think she was trying to tell him something, like maybe she knew something about her dad . . ."

If Mr. Esposito wasn't already convinced, the bracelet seemed to clinch it.

"Not one step closer to that man," he says, finishing his command from earlier. "This isn't for you kids to handle."

We stay at Enzo and Maritza's house until long after the streetlights go on, leaving Mr. Esposito to make some calls on his own, to study the binder in quiet, to pace the floors of the kitchen while we hang out in the basement and pretend not to speculate about what it is he'll decide to do.

We're all reluctant to turn over our stash of evidence to Mr. Esposito, and I'm the hardest to convince. It's not that I don't trust him . . . he's the first adult to actually listen to this whole mess. I pretend to be okay with it, letting him take the binder and the note and the photos and lock them in a drawer in his office before piling us all in his car and taking us home, one by one. My dad is already in bed, and most of me is relieved, but there's still this huge angry elephant in the room because Dad and I haven't really talked since our fight, and I swear I've never felt more alone, even though I have my friends.

Most of my friends.

I pretend to be okay when I wave goodbye to Mr. Esposito, but really, I'm far from it. All this time, I thought it would make me feel better to be heard, to be believed. It's strange, though. Now I feel empty. It's like that binder was covering this huge hole, and now that it's gone, all I feel is drafty.

The dream I have that night doesn't help that feeling go away. I'm in the roller coaster car again with the mannequin.

And this time, we're not alone in the car. This time, Lucy Yi sits next to me. She doesn't breathe a word as we roll slowly to the apex of the impossibly high track. She simply stares straight ahead, resigned to the fate that she knows awaits her at the top. But just as our car begins to level— just before the gut-squeezing drop—she takes my hand and places something cold in my palm.

When I wake up, I'm clutching a gold bracelet, tarnished nearly green, a tiny apple charm dangling from its links.

"What?"

I stare hard at the apple, looking for the tiny divot in the fruit, but it isn't there. Which makes perfect sense, seeing as Lucy's was the one with the dent, and Mr. Esposito has that now, doesn't he?

"Then whose is this?" I ask myself, pinching the skin on my arm to make sure I'm not still dreaming.

"Narf, can you come down here a sec?"

For a second, still trapped in my dream haze, I think my dad must have the answer. He's calling me downstairs to explain. But when I get to the landing, I'm even more confused because Officer Keith and a policewoman are standing in the living room while Mom and Dad hold their coffee mugs and look worried.

Suddenly, my mind is racing.

Dad called the cops on me because I followed Mr. Peterson.

Mr. Peterson knows it was me in the wardrobe.

Mr. Llama knows we hid in his shed.

The list of my crimes is longer than my life.

"Narf, you remember Officer Newsom?" Mom says, lifting an eyebrow over her coffee mug. It takes me a second to understand she's talking about Officer Keith. Then I remember why Officer Newsom and I are already acquainted.

"Uh, yeah," I say, wishing I had my own robe to hide behind.

"The police are here about what you told Mr. Esposito," Dad says, and it's the weirdest thing because I think Dad

177

sounds a little hurt. Like maybe he's bummed I went to Mr. Esposito after our own talk went so wrong.

"Okay," I say, because what else is there to say?

"These are serious allegations, young man," the other police officer says, and it sounds a little strange coming from her because she looks like she could be a senior at Raven Brooks High.

"So you don't believe us," I say rather than ask. I knew it was too good to be true. I had one blissful night of being heard.

This time Dad sounds less hurt and dare I say maybe a little proud. "Oh, no, they're looking into it," he says. "This is serious."

Everyone keeps using that word: "serious." Why are they so surprised about that? It's like they think kids spend their entire day eating Fun Dip, twirling around, and knocking their heads into walls. And granted, that's great (so long as you wear a helmet), but we do have our serious moments, too. Especially when it comes to our friends.

The police repeat the same warnings Mr. Esposito issued the night before about staying away from Mr. Peterson and maintaining a strict curfew. Then my parents add their own warnings:

"No talking to reporters," Dad says, then smiles a little. "Except for me."

"You don't say anything to anyone—*anyone*—without

your dad and me there with you," Mom says, and we all stand up a little straighter when she talks, because as usual, Mom's warning sounds the sternest.

"From now on, we're driving you to school," Dad says, and that sounds like a total drag, but it also feels pretty great to be protected. I didn't realize until this moment it's a feeling that I've missed.

The police leave, and I go over it all with my parents, every last thing we told Mr. Esposito last night: the binder and the pictures, the recorded phone call with Aunt Lisa, the note from Aaron, Lucy's bracelet.

I leave out the bracelet I found in my hand this morning.

Mom hugs me so hard, I think she's going to snap me in half. Then she holds me at arm's length and stares at my face long enough to make me epically uncomfortable. Afterward, she goes to study some compounds because that makes her feel better. Dad goes to his office at the end of the dark hallway because that makes him feel better.

I go upstairs and lie in bed because it's the only way to get my brain to slow down enough to keep my head from pounding.

Just when I think I might start to doze off, I hear the crinkling of a wrapper, and Dad taps lightly on my bedroom door.

He has two Ding Dongs in his hands, and he extends one to me, which I take without a word. I want to accept his peace offering as much as he wants to offer it, which is a lot. We're both done with fighting.

"I'm glad you kids went to someone with all of this," he says. "I think you've had to shoulder a lot these past few months." He swallows the last bite of his Ding Dong and adds, "More than you should have had to shoulder."

I shrug even though it means everything that he just said that.

"I'm just glad people are listening," I say.

"Narf, I feel really bad about the other night," he says, looking down at his long toes curling on the hardwood floors. "I said some things I regret."

"Kinda hard to blame you for saying some of it."

"You know how I get about ice cream," Dad says.

I stop and think about what I say next. "My friends' parents say you're a 'real newsman.'"

Dad smirks. He's never been good at taking compliments.

"What do you think that means?" he asks me, and it's the first time I think Dad's actually asked me what I think of him.

"You tell the truth," I say, and he watches me carefully. Which is why I add, "And the truth isn't just one perspective."

That seems to be good enough for Dad because he slings his arm around my shoulder, and out of nowhere, I start to cry. It's mortifying, and it only happens for a second, but I let it. And Dad lets it. I hiccup a few times, wipe my nose on his sleeve, and shake myself off all over like a dog coming out of the sprinklers.

Dad doesn't even ask.

As he's closing the door behind him, I offer him one more truth.

"I think I want to be an engineer."

He turns back around, smiles the biggest smile I've seen him wear in nearly three months, and says, "Color me surprised."

I hear him chuckle as he walks down the hall and joins my mom in their room.

"An engineer," I hear him say, and he chuckles again.

"Oh God," Mom groans, but I know she doesn't really mean it. "Of *course*, an engineer."

That night, I sleep a deep, dreamless sleep that holds me like a warm, dense blanket.

Chapter 14

It smells like waffles, so everything is starting to feel okay again. The sunlight creeps into my room with the same slowness it has every morning since winter officially arrived, but that's okay. It may be dark, but I can still see, and it may be early, but I slept my first peaceful sleep in what feels like years.

The allure of the waffles is strong, but I know they're not ready yet. Dad always makes the same joke when he makes them, something having to do with breakfast and waffling on my decision about what to eat. Not being the best at puns has never stopped my dad from making them.

He hasn't called to me from the bottom of the stairs yet, so I have a little time.

And maybe it's knowing that I'm not alone in my search for Aaron and Mya anymore, or maybe it's the way I'm already getting used to that drafty hole inside of me that the binder left when I gave it up. Or maybe it's because Dad and I aren't fighting anymore. Whatever it is, I feel braver this morning. Brave enough to look under my bed.

Most kids fear a boogeyman, some disembodied hand to yank them from the depths of their closets or the dark that swallows that space beneath their mattresses. My boogeyman is a tin sign with my name on it, an audio manipulator that still makes the most perfect farting sounds, and a gold-and-flower-covered address book that contains only one number I care about.

I pull out the sign first. I haven't dared to look at it since Aaron disappeared. It looks different now. Smaller, somehow. But it's still magical because it has my name on it and he wanted me to have it. I pull out the audio manipulator and run through its catalog of farts: the Trumpet, the (Mostly) Silent Sly, the Long Smelly Road Home, and, of course, the classic Roaster, each expertly curated by Aaron and me after ingesting a stack of Surviva bars. They sound even better than I remember them.

I reach under the bed for the address book, not kept for any sentimental reason, but because I was so terrified after I got home that afternoon, I threw it under my bed, forgetting to put it with the rest of my collected evidence in my secret drawer. I need to remember to give it to Mr. Esposito the next time I see him.

But no matter which way I swipe my hand under my bed, it only kicks up dust and the occasional crumpled sock. I crawl as far underneath as I can without getting myself stuck, but the little flowered book is nowhere to be found.

I think back on last night. Maybe I did give it to Mr. Esposito after all? The conversation was pretty intense. Maybe I'm not remembering everything. But that doesn't feel right. I remember the rest of what happened so clearly.

"Narf! Syrup or sugar? No waffling!" Dad calls from downstairs.

"Every time, Jay?" I can hear Mom complain as I make my way down the steps, but I know she'd be devastated if his puns suddenly ceased.

I'm just about to lobby for powdered sugar *and* syrup, when the phone rings.

We all stare at it like it's something the Aliens left for us. It's just that no one ever calls this early.

Dad's the first one to snap out of it.

"Oh, Enzo, hi! Hey, how are you doing—?"

Dad's smile slips away.

"Okay. Okay. Just slow down."

I walk across the kitchen, and it feels like the walls are starting to wobble around me. Is this what it feels like right before the bottom falls out of the world? Why isn't Dad talking anymore? Why is he just nodding?

He hangs up before I have a chance to take the phone and ask Enzo myself.

"We need to get over to the police station," he says, and now Mom is across the kitchen, too. "They raided Ted Peterson's house last night."

* * *

Mr. Esposito is already there with Enzo and Maritza, and he and Dad do their quick hug-shoulder-handshake thing before turning to greet Trinity and her parents.

"Been hoping to meet you for a while," my dad says to them, and my mom goes straight in for a hug with Trinity's mom, who, to her credit, doesn't even look surprised by that.

"We're really appreciative of all you've been doing for the community," Mom says.

Trinity's mom smiles warmly. "I'm Joy," she says, and Trinity's dad extends his hand to my dad. "Donald. Pleasure's mine."

They barely have time to make weird grown-up conversation before Officer Keith and the other officer from yesterday morning open the door and usher us back into the squad room, which I expect to have big wooden desks with aluminum filing cabinets and black rotary phones, with hustling cops chasing down leads on hardened criminals.

This looks like an office where they might sell insurance. The cubicles are gray, the phones are a lighter gray, and Officers Newsom and Kornwell are the only ones chasing down leads, and they're not moving fast enough to chase a sloth.

We go into a conference room, where they offer the parents coffee and the kids sodas, which all come in Styrofoam cups with those little red stirring straws, though why soda needs stirring is a mystery to me. Maritza, Enzo, Trinity, and I clump together in the corner and wait for Officer Newsom to come back from the bathroom before we begin.

"Thanks for coming down on such short notice," Officer Kornwell says.

"We're hoping you have more to tell us," says Mr. Esposito.

"We hear you searched his house," Mr. Bales says.

Officer Kornwell nods. "We did."

We all wait silently, and Officer Kornwell dives in.

"We searched the premises on which you reported suspicious activity, namely the residence and the grounds of the former Golden Apple Amusement Park. We did find some old equipment from the park and had a discussion about who owns the rights to the property still contained within the park's limits. We won't be pressing charges, but Mr. Peterson has agreed to return the confiscated items and refrain from visiting the grounds while its ownership is in dispute."

"Um, okay," Maritza says, "but the—the *body* he was unburying? I have a picture!"

The officers turn to each other and share a smile like they have a private joke, and maybe I don't know what the right way is to talk about a guy unearthing a body in front of a bunch of kids, but this feels like the wrong way.

"We investigated that as well," Officer Kornwell says, her voice patronizing. "It was a . . ." And suddenly she's at a loss for words.

"A dummy," Officer Newsom says.

"I'm sorry?" My dad leans an ear in like he couldn't have heard that right.

"A sort of mannequin," Officer Kornwell says. "Probably buried by some kids as a sick joke."

"But why would he be digging it up?" Trinity asks, not letting them get away with their dismissal.

"Who knows?" Officer Newsom says, and it sounds an awful lot like "Who cares?"

"But what about all the TV dinner containers for two, and the funky smell in his house, and the note?" Enzo pleads, and I swear the cops actually look at each other and start to laugh.

"Well, if eating too much and keeping a dirty house are against the law, then I'm in the wrong line of work," Officer Kornwell says.

They seem to gather themselves when they see us all looking at them.

"Right, the note. I'm sorry, but it just doesn't . . . mean anything."

"There was *blood*!" I know I'm raising my voice, and I know that's a terrible idea in front of two police officers and three sets of parents, but Aaron and Mya are missing, Mr. Peterson is free to roam Raven Brooks, we just got finished risking our actual lives to get enough proof to bring to the police, and now they're laughing at us?

Officer Kornwell seems to finally grasp the severity of the situation because any trace of the teasing in her eyes vanishes, and now she just looks sorry for me. "Kids cut themselves all the time. Didn't you say you found the note near a broken window?"

"Well, did you test the blood? Was it Aaron's?" I just can't accept that he gave himself a paper cut.

"We would need a reason to test it," she says, still looking sad for me. "And the note . . . it didn't really say anything to warrant that. Combined with no real crime on Mr. Peterson's end aside from strange behavior . . ."

"Some people are just odd ducks," Officer Newsom surmises.

I look around at my side of the table. Someone, *anyone*, could step in at any point. Where are they? But all the parents, even mine, have that same sad look on their faces now. Only Enzo, Maritza, and Trinity look as unconvinced as me.

Then Maritza's eye widen. "Aunt Lisa!" she shouts, making everyone jump.

Trinity recovers first. "That's right! She doesn't have the kids. She said it herself!"

For the first time this morning, maybe even ever, Officer Kornwell looks like an actual cop instead of a teenager pretending to be one.

"Well, now that's a different ball of wax," he says, and he and Officer Kornwell exchange a grave nod.

"It would appear Aaron and Mya *were* with her, but at some point, they must have run off. She filed a missing persons report around the same time you claimed to have contacted her. We just didn't know about it. Had no real reason to know."

My stomach begins to twist. "Did you . . . did you find them?"

I still expect someone in the room to tell me I'm crazy, but everyone just leans a little closer to the police, waiting for their answer.

"The children?" Officer Newsom seems confused.

"Yes, the children," Mom repeats, and I can tell she's starting to get irritated. It's a side effect of worry for her.

"Well, no, that would be out of our jurisdiction," Officer Newsom says, still looking a little baffled.

"But they're *missing*!" I say, and how can he not understand that?

"Unless we have just cause to believe they're missing here in Raven Brooks, then we have neither the resources nor the legal authority to search for two runaways hundreds of miles away—"

"Mya." My mouth finally forms the words. "She came to me the night before her mom died. She was asking for help."

The officers look hard at me again. "Help with what?"

I fumble for an answer. What did she ask me that night? "She told me her dad was 'getting worse,' but when I asked to get another adult involved, she didn't want that. I didn't think—"

"Young man, if you had suspicion of abuse or neglect, you should have come to us immed—"

"He's the reason they're missing!" I yell, and my mom puts a hand on my arm, but I barely feel it.

Officer Kornwell softens her voice to a whisper. "We have no evidence of that."

She acts like she cares. Maybe she does care. But it means nothing because while Mya and Aaron are missing, they're talking about jurisdiction and authority and resources and a lack of evidence even though there's a boatload of evidence.

Enzo and Trinity try to tell me it's okay. We're in the parking lot waiting for our parents, and they want me to know it isn't over.

"We'll just have to find another way," they say, but I don't believe that. I refuse to have hope. I dared to this time—I dared to think the adults would actually believe us. And for twelve hours, they did. But I can tell when they join us by the cars that the police have won them over. The investigation is finished, not that it ever started. Aaron and Mya are runaways, roaming the forests and lakes of Minnesota and giving their aunt Lisa fits looking for them. And nobody cares that Mr. Peterson doesn't seem to miss them one bit.

"It's not over," Maritza says as we all drift toward our parents' cars, and she sounds as mad as I feel, which only makes me feel slightly better.

On the drive home, I expect my parents to restart the conversation Dad and I began in the driveway the other night—to demand apologies from me for chasing after Mr.

Peterson, for sneaking around late at night, for yelling in the police station. Instead, *they* apologize to *me* for the stress I've felt in losing Aaron and Mya so suddenly, for the strain of starting fresh yet again, for the toll it's taken on my fragile adolescent brain as we've moved from home to home, state to state.

"Officer Kornwell recommended an excellent adolescent counselor," Mom says.

"We'll start off once a week, and you only have to talk about what you feel like talking about," Dad says.

"Maybe we'll join you," Mom says.

"It couldn't hurt," Dad says.

But they have no idea how much it could hurt. They don't now the first thing about hurting.

"Why?" I ask, my voice flat. I can't seem to find an emotion to put behind it. "What's the point? Why would anyone believe what I have to say anyway?"

Mom and Dad spend the rest of the ride home trying to convince me that they do believe me, that they do trust me, that they believe that I believe in Mr. Peterson's guilt.

"But the facts just don't line up, Nicky," Mom says, her voice growing stern. "And we can't have you continuing to harass him. That man's already been put through enough."

And just like that, Mr. Peterson has gone from perpetrator to victim, and I'm never going to see Aaron or Mya again.

* * *

That night, I don't mean to sneak out. It's not like I sat there in the police station this morning or in the car on the way home or in my room for the rest of this miserable day plotting to directly defy my parents' orders and the cops' orders and any reasonable person's orders and leave the safety of my room. It's just that I can't be in my house anymore. The heater's going full blast, and every single wall of my house suddenly feels like bars on a cage.

Outside is freezing, but I can breathe this freezing air easily, and no one is hovering nearby to look worried and ask if I'm okay. Mom and Dad are asleep. The whole town of Raven Brooks is asleep.

I take the long path through the woods, the way I used to walk with Aaron, the one that lets me see just the top of the Ferris wheel, just the distant summit of the Rotten Core. I'm not going to the Golden Apple Amusement Park, though. I'm going to the factory.

I expect to find the fencing and the cameras. I expect to be kept at a far distance, the little Xed-out man threatening to prosecute me if I try climbing the fence. But when I emerge from the overgrowth into the clearing that surrounds the abandoned factory, the camera with its blinking red eye and the fence with the razor wire coiled at the top are gone. A bulldozer sleeps nearby, along with a large crane truck, its hook already armed with a wrecking ball.

I take a cursory glance around and then walk through the doors of what used to be Aaron's place before he shared it with me. Inside, I find it even more barren than it was the first time I saw it. The conveyer belt that once ran half the length of the lower warehouse floor is gone; only a series of bolt holes in the floor stand as witness to its former existence. The corridor of doors is now just a hallway stripped of every locked door, the doorways naked and exposed under the moonlight that streams in through the open ceiling panels. Even the rats seem to have disappeared. Not a single scurry behind the walls matches my movements.

"Every last bit of you is gone," I say to the factory, but I'm saying it to Aaron, and if the rats were still here, even they'd understand that. "How could you be gone just like that?"

There's still one room I haven't checked, though.

The first door leading to the room is gone like the rest, but my heart speeds at the sight of the second door still intact—the one leading to the Office. I grasp the handle and twist, but the knob falls off in my hand. As I push through, I see nothing but utter destruction.

The television monitor is smashed, its face bashed in by the VCR that used to reside next to it; now it lays on the floor in pieces. The filing cabinet that once held our stash of rations is on its side, its middle drawer half open like a tongue above a broken jaw. An unopened soda can peeks from the shadow in the corner, unconvinced that it's safe to come out. The cushy executive chairs where we used to lounge are slashed and gutted, their foam stuffing spilling from the seats and arms.

And by my foot, a VHS tape lies in pieces, its film exposed and shredded. I bend to pick up the piece of its spine that still has some of its label, but something in me already knew it was the Tooth tape, the one that ended not with the classic horror film bloodbath it should have, but with the Peterson family crumbling into a pile of dysfunction and madness as its patriarch took a hammer to their world.

I hold streams of the film to the moonlight, but I already know it's hopeless. The very last bit of evidence there might have been is nothing more than a pile of hard plastic and Mylar.

Less than an hour ago, I couldn't wait to get out of my house, but suddenly I can't wait to be there again. The humming heater, the sheets that trap my feet at the bottom of my bed, the rickety trellis that threatens to break every time I climb it to my window, my snoring parents—now more than ever, these are all things that I want. Because if the entire morning wasn't enough to convince me to give up, finding the Tooth tape has finally done it.

Until one last thought occurs to me.

I don't know why I need to see the tent again. It practically stopped my heart the last time I saw it. But I wasn't expecting it before. The drawings with their terrified little people and the mannequin with its bound hands, all of it was so . . . wrong. Out there in the woods in a corner behind the abandoned factory, none of it should have been there. But the more I dream about roller coasters and faceless, wheeled dummies and greasy machine parts, the more those drawings seem important.

As I run to the overgrown spot, I resolve to take as many drawings as I can carry, and I'll come back for the rest tomorrow. Maybe under better light, I can take a closer look. Maybe I can decipher whatever strange code might reside in those smudgy swipes of pencil lead and ink.

Except I won't be bringing home anything tonight, or any other night. When I turn the corner and look to the tree canopy where the tarp once covered a fort full of drawings, I see nothing but the same overgrowth that's swallowed what remains of anything the Golden Apple Corporation left behind.

"No," I say, because it can't be true.

I stand right in front of the small clearing where there remain only a few slim wisps of fibrous twine knotted to the branches that used to prop up the canvas tarp.

"No!"

I kick a tree trunk hard enough to make my bones rattle all the way up to my knee, which just makes me angrier, so I kick at a huge pile of fallen pinecones, and I know how I'd look if anyone could see a twelve-year-old kid having a tantrum out in the middle of the woods, but this was it. This was my very last idea. This was the only thing left that might have led me to Aaron and Mya—the only shred of evidence that there was something going on in these woods, something that a whole lot of someones seem to want to erase, or at least don't seem to care enough to keep.

I'm not crying. It's just sweat dripping in my eyes, and that burns, so my eyes are watering.

I'm not crying. And anyway, who cares if I am? It's not like there's anyone there to see me do it.

"You win, Universe," I say, choking back angry tears, and I run home. I run until my legs ache and my cheeks burn with wind and cold, and my lungs struggle to keep full. I run until I can't hear the sound of that little voice in my head that tells me to keep searching, that Aaron and Mya can be found, that they even want to be found. I run until the thumping in my ears is nothing more than my pounding heart, and the questions and suspicions and fears turn to certainties: I will never find them.

And I'm done looking.

I climb the trellis slowly, partly because I'm afraid it will break this time, and partly because I'm just too tired to climb it any faster. I leave my window open with the screen over it because I'm hot after running, and I'm so tired of feeling afraid.

I find the little golden apple bracelet on my bed, right where I left it, and I'm done wondering whose it is and how I came to be holding it so tightly in my fist when I woke up. So I throw it hard across the room, letting it skitter to the floor in some forgotten corner.

When I crawl into bed, I pull the comforter hard over my head, letting the air slowly run out underneath the tent I've made, waiting until the last possible second to come back to the surface for an inhale.

Then, ever so quietly, I hear something outside. At first, I think maybe it's a bird, but that can't be right because it's the middle of the night in winter. I listen harder; slowly, a tune begins to emerge. A tune I recognize immediately.

He whistles it at first, then begins to sing.

> *"Tom, Tom, the piper's son,*
> *Stole a pig and away did run.*
> *The pig was eat, and Tom was beat,*
> *And Tom went howling down the street."*

I walk slowly to the window, but I don't bother to sneak up on it. He already knows I'm here.

There in the middle of the street, his hands behind his back, his mustache curled high, is Mr. Peterson, fully clothed for daytime, black grease smears staining his khaki pants. Once he's sure I'm watching, he pulls one grease-streaked hand from behind his back and holds up a gold-and-flowered address book, waving it back and forth like a dainty fan.

Then, without another word, without a whistle or a smile, he turns slowly on his heel and walks casually back into his house, disappearing behind the front door. I stand at my window for so long, my legs begin to tremble, and I want to believe it's exhaustion, but then I hear music again, this time coming from the basement across the street—the carnival music I've heard on more nights than I can count, coming from the bowels of the Peterson house.

And even though I close my window and lock it, and even though I slide my dresser in front of it, no level of barricade feels safe tonight. Because if Mr. Peterson was holding that address book, he got it from my room. This time, the threat of him is clearer than the tune of his whistled lullaby.

This time, there really is a boogeyman. And he's been under my bed.

About the Author

Photo credit: Kristyn Stroble

CARLY ANNE WEST is the author of the YA novels *The Murmurings* and *The Bargaining*. She holds an MFA in English and Writing from Mills College and lives with her husband and two kids near Portland, Oregon. Visit her at www.carlyannewest.com.